Echoes from the Same House

Echoes from the Same House

86 Brand New Short Stories
That'll Catch You By Surprise

Jeff W. Linzey • Christopher J. Linzey
Kevin M. Linzey • Paul E. Linzey

Echoes from the Same House

ISBN: 979-8-9985060-9-3

DEDICATION

Jeff: For my father, whose love, support, and steady belief in me have helped shaped every chapter of my life. Thank you for inspiring our shared writing journey and for being a great source of courage and encouragement.

Kevin: To my dad, brothers, and sons. You inspire me to be the best man I can be. And to my mom, thanks for ~~putting up with~~ . . . ~~enduring~~ . . . loving the Linzey men!

Chris: To my family, without whom I wouldn't be who I am today.

Paul: To my three sons. Your friendship and partnership go way beyond the scope of this project, but it was fun doing this with you.

CONTENTS

CONTENTS

CONTENTS

INTRODUCTION

Families speak in rhythms long before they speak in words. Before any of us could form sentences, we were already learning the cadence of our shared life—the hum of a house full of stories, the rustle of pages turning in the next room, the laughter that traveled down hallways, the quiet comfort of knowing someone else was awake. Those early sounds became our first language, a kind of pre-verbal harmony that shaped us long before we knew we were being shaped.

We grew up in a world built by two parents who believed in imagination, curiosity, and the occasional well-timed joke. Our childhood home was not grand, but it was rich in the things that matter: books stacked in corners, conversations that stretched past bedtime, and a sense that creativity was not a hobby but a way of moving through the world. Three sons learned to navigate that landscape—sometimes together, sometimes in parallel, sometimes in competition over who got the last Pop-Tart, scoop of ice cream, or got to eat all of the chips that remained in the bag. And through it all, a father watched, guided, and occasionally refereed.

Eventually, of course, we grew up. Life scattered us into different cities, different careers, different orbits. One of us became analytical, another adventurous, another introspective. The father accumulated years of perspective, watching his sons become men with their own stories to tell. Our lives diverged, our experiences branched outward, and our voices developed their own timbre. Yet something of that early music stayed with us, a resonance that never fully faded.

This anthology began with a simple idea—simple in theory, anyway. A father and his three sons would take a list of writing prompts and respond to them independently. No comparing drafts. No coordinating themes. No arguing over who stole whose idea. Just four people, connected by history but separated by circumstance, writing their way through the same creative challenges.

The prompts ranged from the playful to the profound. "Write a story in one sentence." "Write about a parent and child." "Write about a traveler." Some were invitations to be clever, others to be vulnerable, others to be strange. Each prompt was a doorway, and each of us walked through it in our own way. What emerged was not a single narrative but a constellation—four points of light connected by invisible lines of memory.

If you've ever wondered what happens when a family attempts a creative project together, the answer is: a surprising amount of laughter, a few debates about commas, and a shared document that looked like a family reunion collided with a creative writing workshop. There was enthusiasm, mild confusion, and at least one person asking, "Wait, what are we doing again?" But beneath the chaos was something steady and familiar—a sense of togetherness that felt like returning to a childhood room and finding the wallpaper unchanged.

What ties these stories together isn't uniformity—it's origin. They spring from shared roots, even if the branches twist in different directions. They are variations on a theme, harmonies built on the same chord. They are echoes of the same early rhythms, refracted through the lives we've lived since leaving that childhood home.

Some stories in this collection are sharp and concise; others sprawling and contemplative. Some are humorous, others tender, others strange in the best possible way. They don't match, and they're not meant to. Instead, they resonate. They bounce off one another. They reveal the ways in which four people can look at the same prompt and see four entirely different worlds—yet still feel connected by something deeper than style or structure.

Think of this anthology as four flashlights shining on the same object from different angles. Or four voices calling out from different rooms, their tones distinct but their origins unmistakably intertwined. These pieces are, in every sense, echoes from the same house—familiar in tone, varied in shape, each of its own tenor (though at least two are more baritone).

If you listen closely, you may hear the harmony beneath the differences. Or you may simply enjoy the contrast. Either way, we hope you find something here that lingers, the way echoes do. Something that reminds you of your own family's rhythms, your own shared beginnings, your own branching paths.

This book is not just a collection of stories. It is a testament to the strange, beautiful alchemy of family: how people can grow up together, scatter into the world, and still find themselves connected by invisible threads. It is a celebration of individuality shaped by togetherness, of voices that diverge yet still resonate with one another.

Most of all, it is a reminder that no matter how far we travel—across cities, across careers, across the shifting landscapes of our lives—we carry the early echoes with us. They shape us, steady us, surprise us. And sometimes, if we're lucky, they bring us back to one another in unexpected ways.

We hope you enjoy these stories. We hope you hear the kinship in them. And we hope that, somewhere in these pages, you find a reflection of your own echoes—soft, distinct, intertwined—carried forward by time and transformed by experience.

Jeff W. Linzey

Echoes from the Same House

1

THE 6' 11" BALLERINO

Maurice "Ticket Scalper" Cagey was a physical paradox wrapped in a size XXXL jersey. At 6'11" and 250 pounds of chiseled muscle, he was a specimen of athletic potential. He could outrun the team's point guard, out-jump their center, and bench press the entire coaching staff. His one, glaring, comically oversized flaw? The man had feet for hands and hands for feet. He was, to put it kindly, profoundly clumsy.

His nickname, "Ticket Scalper," was a gift from the team's sarcastic benchwarmers. Every time Maurice touched the ball on offense, the entire arena held its breath, paying the full price of admission with their frayed nerves. You never knew if you were about to witness a highlight-reel miracle or a man attempting to dribble with his knees while taking a seven-step scenic tour of the lane.

Maurice, however, saw himself as a misunderstood offensive virtuoso. In his mind, he was a graceful giant, a maestro of the post-move, unfairly persecuted by referees who just couldn't appreciate his avant-garde interpretation of the rulebook.

With ten seconds left in a tied game, the ball swung to Maurice on the right wing. A collective groan rippled through the home crowd. The opposing defender, a wiry kid who looked like he'd just lost a fight with a lawnmower, cautiously gave Maurice six feet of space, practically begging him to travel.

Maurice's eyes lit up. This was it. His moment.

He caught the ball and faced his opponent, planting his right foot as a pivot. The crowd braced for the inevitable shuffle. But this time felt different. Maurice took a deep breath, channeling every YouTube instructional video he'd ever watched at 2x speed.

He began his dance.

First, a sharp jab step with his left foot. *Bam!* The floor squeaked. The defender didn't flinch. Maurice pulled the foot back. He then executed a second, more theatrical jab step, this time with a head fake that nearly sent his own headband flying into the stands. The defender blinked.

Now for the pivot. Maurice imagined he was a ballerina. A very, very large, sweaty ballerina. He swung his left leg around in a wide, graceful arc, his size-15 sneaker hovering inches above the polished wood. He pivoted on his right foot, a full 180-degree spin, his body a blur of red and white. He was a tornado of athletic ineptitude, and it was mesmerizing. The defender, caught completely off guard by the sheer audacity of the move, took a half-step back in confusion.

That was the opening.

Out of the clumsy, chaotic pirouette, Maurice suddenly exploded forward. He put the ball on the floor for one, powerful, and, most importantly, *"legal"* dribble. He took two thunderous steps, his sneakers pounding the floor like war drums, covering the distance to the hoop in an instant. He launched himself into the air, a human wrecking ball soaring toward the rim.

With a primal roar, he slammed the ball through the hoop so hard the entire backboard shuddered, and the net snapped upwards as if in surrender.

The buzzer sounded. The crowd erupted, but their cheers were laced with a question. Every single person in the gym—players, coaches, fans, the hot dog vendor in the lobby—instantly turned their heads to stare at the referee under the basket.

The ref, a veteran with a look of permanent exhaustion, stood frozen for a beat. He squinted, replaying the sequence in his mind: the jab, the jab, the bizarrely elegant-yet-awkward pirouette, the single dribble, the two steps. He recalled Maurice's planted pivot foot, which, by some miracle of physics and dumb luck, had remained perfectly anchored to the floor like it was bolted down.

After a moment that felt like an eternity, the ref simply shrugged, blew his whistle, and emphatically signaled a good basket.

Maurice Cagey, the Ticket Scalper, stood under the hoop, chest puffed out, a look of pure, unadulterated triumph on his face. He had finally done it. He had created a masterpiece of footwork. And for once, the ticket was worth every single penny.

2

AFTER MATH

Anders had always known his writing was strange. Flash fiction about talking animals wasn't exactly a booming market, but it was the only thing that ever felt like his voice. He arranged his collected works into what he believed was the perfect sequence, though half still lacked titles. Of the few pieces he'd published, even fewer had earned more than token payments. His biggest success was a 1,500-word fantasy called *Math,* which Clarkesworld bought for a little over two hundred dollars. The story's quirky premise — animals in the sprawling forest of "Arithmos" living by ancient principles known as "Math": Addition, Subtraction, Division, and Multiplication — earned him a sliver of notoriety among friends, and he shared its summary with anyone willing to listen.

But the story he believed in most — the one he quietly hoped might outlive him — was the one he still called *After Math,* stylizing it like the first century A.D. editor who assembled the treatise we know as Aristotle's Metaphysics. He'd researched and rewritten it obsessively, weaving emotion with a surprisingly accurate history of Military Working Dogs. Unlike his earlier attempts at giving antagonists meaningful lessons, this one let the underdog win — and offered a moral that wasn't just a counterpoint to the villain's, but something gentler, deeper.

He had written it during a time when he himself felt like an imposter, unsure whether his work mattered to anyone. Maybe that was why he'd poured so much of his own doubt — and his own hope — into the Labrador at the heart of the story.

* * *

"You're not a real service dog," Brutus scoffed. The Belgian Malinois, a decorated Military Working Dog, towered over Shadow, a young Labrador Retriever certified as an emotional support animal.

Shadow had been trying to help a nervous child in the waiting room only moments earlier, but Brutus's voice cut through her confidence like a cold wind.

Dutch, a broad-chested German Shepherd from SWAT, added, "He's rude, but he's not wrong. At least other Labs get trained for narcotics, explosives, or search and rescue. Emotional support? That's barely service work."

Shadow's tail faltered. She knew she was a good girl — she *felt* it when people's breathing steadied under her touch — but their words made her feel small.

Brutus and Dutch were legends in the working-dog world, known for their skill and their disdain for what they called "Soft Service." They respected Seeing Eye Dogs, but emotional support animals ranked at the bottom of their hierarchy.

Shadow swallowed hard. "I help people," she said quietly. "Just . . . in a different way."

Dutch snorted, but something in his eyes flickered — not quite agreement, but not dismissal either.

Brutus launched into a sweeping monologue about the history of Military Working Dogs: their ancient origins, their evolution into highly trained partners, their unmatched senses, their heroism in war. Dutch settled into a commanding sit and ordered Shadow to do the same, his tone dismissive but his posture betraying a grudging respect for Brutus's storytelling.

Brutus spoke of early combat dogs, of the War Dog Program of 1942, of legendary canines like Chips — the German Shepherd mix who attacked a machine-gun nest in Italy. Dutch rose, circled to ease his stiff joints, then resumed a stance that radiated authority. Shadow listened, awed and increasingly aware of how little she knew about her own role in the world.

But she also noticed something else: Brutus's voice softened when he spoke of the dogs who never came home. There was pride there, yes — but also grief.

As Brutus's speech wound down, a young man shuffled past them, shoulders slumped, eyes hollow.

Dutch sat immediately — his drug-detection training signaling a near-certain hit. Brutus tensed, ready for confrontation.

Shadow stepped forward before she could talk herself out of it.

She nudged the man's hand. He paused, then knelt, resting his forehead briefly against hers. A thin, aching smile crossed his face as a tear slipped down his cheek.

"Thanks, sweetie," he whispered. "I really needed that."

Shadow's tail wagged softly, pride blooming in her chest. Brutus and Dutch watched in silence. Joy and tenderness had been trained out of them long ago — but not forgotten.

Dutch exhaled, long and low. "Huh," he murmured. "Didn't think . . . well. Good work."

Brutus didn't speak, but his ears dipped — the smallest nod of respect.

Shadow stayed a moment longer, basking in the quiet certainty of her purpose.

* * *

Anders's alpha readers loved the concept but pointed out structural gaps and character inconsistencies. His beta readers — members of his target audience — helped him refine pacing and dialogue. One suggested renaming *After Math* to *Beyond Shadow's Doubt*, and Anders immediately knew it was right.

He realized, reading their notes, that he had written Shadow's journey to understand his own: that value isn't measured by the loudest accomplishments, but by the quiet moments when someone truly needs you.

With a few final tweaks, he felt satisfied. Now he only had thirty-nine untitled stories left — and the daunting task of figuring out how to publish them.

But for the first time in a long while, he didn't doubt himself.

Not beyond Shadow's doubt.

3

ANIMAL CONTROL

I hate being pigeon-holed. I am more than what you see when you look at me. I am more than my outward appearance. Blondes are dumb. Blondes are silly. Blondes are just there for a fun time but there's not much upstairs.

If all you see is my golden yellow hair, then you are not seeing the real me. The fighter. The survivor. The one who faces insane wildlife in their natural habitat and lives to tell the tale.

It's not as though I went looking for the sleuth of bears. I bet you didn't even know that's what you call a group of bears, did you? I didn't think so.

Okay, fine.... I'll be honest. I had to look it up after my encounter with them. All I knew is that encountering bears in the wild is crazy dangerous! All you hear about is their side of the story.

PROPAGANDA!

Sure, I happened to stumble into their den. That really wasn't my fault. I signed up for this wilderness nature retreat to "find myself" and "learn about the outdoors." Hoo-boy. I do NOT recommend. First of all, our wilderness guide was this idiot college kid who was just there for a summer job. He really knew nothing about the wilderness, or wildlife, or really anything at all. The trek could have been led by a sixth grader with an iPhone. That's how useless our guide was.

Within the first 45 minutes of hiking – HE WAS LOST! They had been telling us all day, "Make sure to hydrate!" So naturally, being a rule-follower, I had been drinking my water! And what are the natural consequences of hydrating? You have to pee! Oh, I had to go so bad.

I TOLD that kid leading the hike that I had to go. Of course I didn't want to be seen. It's hard enough being a minor celebrity on social media, but to be with a group of people live? I could see the way they all stared at me. "Oh, it's the famous girl with the bright yellow hair! Oh, look, it's Goldilocks!" Naturally I had to go a little distance away so I could take care of my business without the prying eyes of the public.

After hiking up my britches and walking back to where I left that idiot kid…I mean, wilderness guide…the nature exploration group was nowhere to be found. I had a brief moment of panic, and I called out for them until my throat hurt! Wouldn't you know, my phone had no signal there. I tried to make my way back to where I thought we had come from. I got totally lost.

That's what happens when you put a city girl in the middle of the woods.

After a while, it started to rain. It was awful! I was soaked to the bone. Fortunately, I stumbled upon a cave that seemed a good place to wait until I dried off. How was I to know that it was inhabited by a sleuth of bears! Three bears, to be exact. And they were none too friendly.

I stayed as calm as I could. I backed away slowly and used my most relaxed tone. It didn't seem to work. All three bears, the two bigger ones and the one smallish bear, started to growl and roar at me. Me! I hadn't done anything.

Just then my phone dinged. I had finally wandered into an area that had (limited) signal. Just my luck! After a quick Google search, I called the county's animal control hotline. They had an officer only 20 minutes away! Before I knew it, Officer Oso showed up with his tranquilizer gun and the three bears were quickly put to sleep.

While the experience was harrowing, and I will never again participate in a wilderness retreat, I often visit the zoo to see those three bears. At least I didn't ask for them to be put down.

I am not a monster, despite what you may have heard.

4

THE ANNIVERSARY

One year down.
12 months.
365 days.
Jerry had to do the math…
8760 hours.

Of course, thanks to the Broadway show Rent, literally everyone knew how many minutes that was.

Still – it felt significant. Jerry couldn't believe it had been a full year since he had taken a drink. His sponsor, Greg, had given him an anniversary chip tonight. Everyone clapped. Some whistled. Others hooted. Jerry had felt good in the moment – proud of himself.

Then everyone went home to their families, and Jerry went home to an empty apartment. It's not that he blamed Jess. There was no bitterness there. She took off when it was clear that his love for the drink outweighed his love for his family.

One year sober. Two years living alone, watching his kids grow up on social media. He slowly gazed around his threadbare apartment. His loveseat. His lamp. His television. It felt so bare compared to the life had before everything turned to crap.

Not her fault, he reminded himself. This was on me.

He breathed in deeply. In his mind, he could smell the notes of vanilla and honey and oak that were in his favorite bourbon. He imagined the golden-brown liquid and a single ice cube gently swirling around his glass.

He sighed a single, heavy sigh, picked up the phone and made the call.

"Greg? It's Jerry. Yeah, just having a rough night."

5

APATHY AND ELEVATORS

Walter always did well in school, especially math, but had no particular ambitions to steer him in any particular direction. During his senior year at Reading Sr. High School in Pennsylvania, he participated in a trip to NYC. What caught his attention wasn't the plethora of monuments and skyscrapers; rather, it was what was inside most of those large buildings. For reasons he couldn't explain, he found himself fascinated by the elevators. Thinking nothing of it at the time, they finished their two-day excursion in the city, and started heading back to Reading, PA.

The bus ride back was perhaps the biggest indicator of the general ambition and expectation among his peer group. Somehow, the conversation steered toward the subject of what people were going to do after graduating.

"I'm already working at Home Depot. There are opportunities to promote or move to different positions.

They even said if I want to transfer to a different store, that's an option."

"I'm going to do the Nurse Tech program and work in the hospital."

"I work at Walmart. My mom needs a lot of help around the house with my younger siblings, so I'll just keep doing that and help out as much as I can."

"I'm enrolling into Reading Area Community College. Hopefully I can get into Alvernia University after that"

"I got a job as Boscov's. They said if I get my diploma and am willing to work the busy hours, I might be able to move from being a stocker to working on the floor."

"My dad's a manager at a Penske. I'm going to work for him."

When attention fell on Walter and it was his turn to chime in about his post-high school ambitions, his eyes darted to each of his peers. Even though their ambitions were low, at least they had something in mind.

"I don't know. I haven't really thought about it much."

In fact, Walter hadn't thought about it at all. He could always figure it out later. In the meantime, there were daily achievements to unlock on some of his favorite mobile games. When he got tired of whittling away his time with those, he leaned his head against the bus window and watched as they passed fields, pastures, houses, and all manner of routine things that had no potential bearing on his future. Things didn't look great.

At a mandatory session with the guidance counselor going into his final month before graduating, Walter was pressed to answer the question of what he was going to do. She wasn't going to let him go until she got an answer.

"Walter—if you could do anything in the world . . . within reason . . . what would it be?

"Well . . ." his voice petered out, his gaze fell lazily around the room, as if an answer or at least some motivation was somewhere lying around that he might find. "I kind of like elevators."

"Elevators? That's your plan? Elevators?"

"I guess. I mean . . . is that a thing? Can I, like, do . . . elevators?

"Hang on, let me see." Punching away with her thumbs on her smartphone, the counselor's posture froze with her eyes fixed on her little screen. "Well I'll be.... It would appear that there's a low barrier to entry to work as an elevator technician. It's pretty dangerous, kind of like being a lineman, but not really much more dangerous than working at a steel mill."

And like that, Walter found himself well on his way to a 6-figure, dead-end job in the city. Plenty of physical demands, not a lot of social interaction required, and a starting salary of $90k—almost triple what everyone else on the earlier bus trip was looking at.

And so, after graduation, Walter found a small place in the city, and worked.

That amount of money for a young kid in the city is a great way to get in trouble. But with as little motivation and as few interests as Walter had, he spent most nights at karaoke bars or going to shows in town.

His apathy and loneliness were quickly turning into depression, and he knew what he was doing wasn't sustainable. But what else was there? "Nothing Really Matters!"

That thought kept running through his mind. Even at work, while rewiring the elevators or working on the hydraulics that prevent cars of people from plummeting 30 floors to a crushing death, or entire buildings from going up in flames . . . "Nothing really matters." He knew this was becoming precarious. But what?

The show he attended that weekend featured "Queen Nation," the premier Queen tribute band in the world. It was a high-energy escape from the monotony of his dead-end, repetitive, and dangerous-yet-non-exhilarating job. The jolt of enthusiasm he felt at the show was different. He used that energy the following night at karaoke and even enlisted the support of some of his regular rivals to join him for a rendition of Bohemian Rhapsody. They crushed it! And the whole bar's uproarious standing ovation sealed the deal. Walter finally felt excited about something... motivated even. For the first time in as long as he could remember, he had a dream. Taking to the internet that night, he Googled "How to Join a Queen Tribute Band."

The application process was grueling. The competition for limited positions fierce. The auditions looming. Just getting a manager of a legit Queen tribute was difficult, and the few friends in his life challenged why he would jeopardize or throw away his steady, high-income job for such a weird dream. He left those naysayers behind.

The most exciting lead was for a group out of Australia. Well-reputed across the globe, and performing all over (at least all over Australia)... that could be fun.

Didn't pan out.

There were a few other opportunities, but the only response—if he even got one—was rejection (sometimes in harsher words than others).

Walter didn't fancy himself as the greatest Freddie Mercury of all time, but he was finally motivated about something, and ready to work for it. He watched all the footage. Took piano lessons. Practiced replicating the specific sounds, vocal harmonies, and mannerisms of rock's greatest frontman.

A rare opportunity arose with "Bohemian Queen," not only one of the premier tribute bands, but particularly renowned for their 100% live performances of Bohemian Rhapsody. Walter took it as a sign. From that night during karaoke when he stoked his fire and passion in life, he was a man on a mission, and this was the divine confirmation he was doing what he was meant to do.

The audition was nothing short of doing Bohemian Rhapsody from start to finish with Bohemian Queen themselves!!!

The lights, the stage . . . the only audience was the manager sitting near the front and the bandmates on stage. This was the moment on which his entire future hung.

Walter could feel himself channel the spirit of Freddie Mercury into his performance. He was on fire, and nailing every note. His use of the mic stand, his actions on the keys as he tickled the ivories. He was doing it.

". . . Nothing really matters . . . to me."

The manager, whose chilled introduction and stone-cold demeanor did little to instill confidence, now had a subtle smile across his face.

6

THE BACH BANDITS

Bernie and Max had been roommates in college. Bernie was a music major. He played cello. Max majored in computer science. They hadn't planned on a life of crime. I mean, who ever goes into being a thief with the childhood thought of *that's what I want to be when I grow up*. They had kind of stumbled into it one night in their dorm. Bernie was practicing for the next performance of the school's philharmonic. Max was sitting across the room working on his programming project. As Max was playing he heard a loud clunk. He turned around and Max was sprawled out on the floor unconscious. Bernie got up with a start and rushed to his friend.

You ok buddy?

Max slowly came around. Whoaaa! What happened?

I don't know! You just passed out! Did you stay up all night or something studying?

No, man, I'm always good about getting sleep so I'm ready for class!

When was the last time you ate something? Maybe you have low blood sugar?

No, man I just ate like an hour ago.

Weird!

Neither of them thought much of it and so they shook it off and went back to work on practice and coding.

Then about five minutes later . . . clunk!

Max was out again on the floor!

Bernie didn't move this time. He just yelled for his friend to wake up.

As Max sat up on the floor Bernie decided to try something. He played the exact same section of music he had played just before. Max fell back to the floor.

Whoaaa…

When Max woke up Bernie told him what had happened. They looked at each other and laughed! And so it all started as a party joke. They would get friends over for food and games. Bernie would tell everyone he wanted to show them a piece of music he'd been working on. Max would secretly put in earplugs. When their friends zonked out, Max would mess with them while Bernie made sure to keep playing so they kept sleeping. It would start with just moving things around the room. Then moving people around to different areas of the room. Or putting objects on them and then letting them wake up bewildered.

They would never tell their friends what happened but just that it was a magic trick. But they realized… it was the exact right frequency that when it hit people's ears, would basically shut off their conscious brain.

And then Max's dad got sick. He couldn't work. Max's parents couldn't pay for his college anymore. And Max certainly couldn't afford it. One night as the friends wracked their brains for what to do they saw on the news that Amazon had just come out with an in-home smart speaker called Alexa. You could connect it to your lights. Connect it to your computer… but most importantly, you could talk to it and tell it to play music. Millions of songs on the internet not even just at the touch of a button… but at a simple verbal request.

Max, what if we recorded the right frequency and put it on the internet so Alexa could access it? We could knock out anyone in the country! But they couldn't just yell for Alexa in someone else's house. So Max used his skills to create a remote control that could hack the wifi of houses and connect to any Amazon device. They didn't want to hack Amazon itself because they knew the huge company would track them down and find them. So Max figured out a localized wifi override.

And so it began. The friends would scout out a neighborhood to see who got lots of Amazon packages. Those were the most likely people to also have an Alexa device. Then they'd put in earplugs and dress as pizza delivery, or even better Amazon delivery. As the unwitting Amazon customers came to the door Max would trigger his remote and as the front lock clicked open they would hear a thump on the inside as the homeowner collapsed on the floor. The pair of techno thieves marched into the house and took whatever they wanted. They could walk around as long as they liked because they had recorded a five-hour-long "song" of the sleep frequency.

They would never have been caught either except that they didn't pay attention to the next development in music technology after Alexa. One day they were breaking into a house… they heard the thump behind the door and opened it. They strolled in confidently and began to look around when from at the top of the stairs they heard "who the heck are you guys?" They turned in disbelief, wondering how someone could be awake with their scientifically crafted harmonics. At the top of the stairs stood a teenager with brand new Bose noise cancelling headphones on, holding his phone. He immediately held up the phone..."I'm livestreaming punks, you're toast!"

And thus came the end to the Bach Bandits.

7

BALANCE

The porcelain felt cool on the boy's skin. The thrumming of the off-balance vent fan, normally a nuisance to him, was now a symphony to his ears, comforting him. These were the only sensations he was allowing himself to feel. His eyes squeezed tightly shut with the writhing contortions of his belly, so sight wasn't an option. The foul stench in his nostrils wasn't something that couldn be avoided or ignored, hence his fixation on the porcelain and the vent fan. But even those sensations weren't enough. That odor permeated everything. It was the smell of sick. It was the smell of his stomach in rebellion. It was the smell of his lack of self-control.

He tried to blame his parents, but the blame wouldn't stick – even in his own young mind. His mom and dad had always been his own personal harmony, the balance in the Force like Obi-Wan had taught Luke. His personal Yin and

Yang. Dad was always there to say YES! Mom was always there to balance with NO!

Of course, who DOESN'T like to hear YES!? It's the answer every child wants to hear from their parents. It's the universal permission slip to engage in whatever childhood schemes the imagination could dream up. YES! You may go play with your friends. YES! You may have dessert before dinner tonight. YES! You may play video games and do your homework later. YES! You may stay up past your bedtime because you have no tests tomorrow.

YES was everything a boy could want – everything a boy could dream. And Dad was YES.

But always bringing balance, the Yang to the Dad's Yin, was Mom's NO.

NO was the anchor that dragged down the soul that yearned to fly free. NO was the disappointment that reminded of obligations when life wanted to run carefree. NO was the downer that prevented little boys from experiencing the fullness of life that was available if only they could find a way to YES.

Lying there, trying to find solace in the porcelain and vent fan, the boy now realized that NO was the voice of moderation. NO was the voice of reason. NO was the voice of wisdom that could only be appreciated after the fact, when your cheek was pressed hard against the toilet bowl and your eyes were clenched tight and you were fighting for your life every time your stomach revolted against you.

It had been a holiday treat. Mom and Dad had taken him to the ice cream parlor for a cone, and the shop had eggnog ice cream! After the cone was devoured, the boy requested another. Yin and Yang. Balance in the Force.

YES won that round.

So, the boy absolutely destroyed a second ice cream cone of that delectable eggnog ice cream. But the boy knew he was on a roll. He could see that chance was on his side, that Yin was leading the charge, so he asked for one more cone.

Yin and Yang.

Balance in the Force.

YES. NO.

Self-control is the worst, especially for a little boy. When the forces of nature are divided above you, what chance does a kid have?

YES. NO.

This time, YES won. Three times in a row! What luck. He must have been the luckiest kid in the universe. At least, that's what he thought in the moment. Another one!

Just One. More. Cone.

FLUSH!

The porcelain felt cool on the boy's skin . . .

Somewhere outside the bathroom, Mom quietly muttered, "I told you so."

8

BANANAS

"Frivolous, I tell you. No truth at all."

"But Mark, people in different places, even on different continents, have experienced it, and they describe it exactly the same. How do you explain that?"

"I don't have to explain it, Fran. It's just preposterous. C'mon! Be reasonable. There's no such thing. Get real."

They'd only been dating a few weeks when the local news station started reporting about people who were found with what looked like their ears melted off the side of their head, eyes shriveled up to about half their normal size, and most of their skin peeled off.

Rumors varied greatly as to what kind of monster was doing this—everything from beasts that flew, to hideous creatures that followed you and attacked when you were alone—but nobody knew.

When Mark showed up at her condo Friday night for

their date, Fran didn't answer the door. He must have rung the doorbell seven or eight times before deciding to call her. Still no answer. He went around back and found the door unlocked. He opened the door and called out her name. Nothing. So he walked in. There in the hall was Fran.

After vomiting, he called 9-1-1.

Fourteen months went by. A year and two months of continued reports around the world, only now, Mark was a believer because he had seen it. He was heart-broken to have lost Fran. Then one day he happened to turn on CNN. Scientists had discovered deadly, microscopic flesh-eating bacteria that lived only in bananas.

Fran loved bananas.

9

BARSTOOL RACONTEUR

It was a brisk twenty-one degrees outside of the Downunder Sports Pub at the Shiretown Inn and Suites. A local regaled a detoured trucker while emergency workers cleared a major accident that was impeding cross-border traffic with Canada.

"It was one of the coldest winters Maine had seen in nearly a hundred years. Sarah, born and raised in northern Vermont, absolutely loved it. Meanwhile, her husband Dylan was from Miami. How they met is a story for another time, but after getting married and struggling to make ends meet the first couple of years, they made a bet. Sarah won, and they cut ties in South Carolina and headed north along I-95 until they couldn't head north anymore.

They arrived here in Houlton, Maine, quickly found work, and established a reasonable life, making a combined $36k per year. Now, before you lambast my use of the word "reasonable" for such a meager wage, you have to realize that it's slightly higher than the median income in the area. For a young couple like Dylan and Sarah, they lucked out. Dylan worked construction, and Sarah was a sales associate, which worked out well, since childcare in Houlton isn't exactly ideal.

Did I not mention their children? Noah was born the year before they got married, and Evelyn the year afterward. Ohhh . . . don't look at me like that. They're an American family, completely monogamous, love each other, and life happened. Certainly they're not the first couple you've ever heard of having a kid before getting married. At least they got married, you know?

Anyway, where was I? Vermont . . . the bet . . . I-95 . . . the kids. Yes, Sarah's job as a sales associate was somewhat flexible, but dropping Noah off at preschool and getting Evelyn over to the daycare made her late most days. Nevertheless, they found a way.

Which brings us to their first winter in Maine, and the coldest that anyone living in Aroostook County had ever experienced. Their neighbor across the street was Old Man Charles, a crotchety old coot that had lived in northern Maine since a boy when his family moved here so his dad could run the airbase in support of the war effort (World War II—maybe you've heard of it. If not, look it up).

Old Man Charles came across hard, but deep down, he meant well. He told you how wrong you were in everything you did because if he didn't look after you and tell you, harsh winters in Houlton could be the end of things. He even helped repair the used generator that Dylan purchased for back-up power in the late fall.

Old Man Charles was a widower since his wife passed in the summer of 2001. Something about Lyme Disease if memory serves correct. Anyway, sad little life, telling everyone what's what and mostly keeping to himself.

Well, he practically saved their lives. In the middle of December, this trucker was making a run up to Canada and lost control, slamming into a power transformer in a crazy display of sparks and hissing wires. No kidding, there I was in the diner, looking out the window and nursing my coffee before going on shift, and wham! Out of the blue, this 18-wheeler just plows into the transformer and it goes off like the 4th of July.

Talk around town was to the tune of him being drunk behind the wheel, but the police let him go the next day, so who knows. But that transformer going down knocked out power for five whole city blocks.

Dylan and Sarah's place was within that area, and when the power dropped, their heater went out, too. The weather was too dicey to have driven anywhere, but he fired up the generator and got the heat going again. They still huddled the family together in the living room and made sure to have all of their cold-weather gear just in case the generator sputtered and died, but they were fine.

Meanwhile, across the street, Old Man Charles had fallen asleep in his Lazy Boy probably right before all this went down. They found him inside his house, frozen stiff, when checking on the neighborhood the next day. He had a well-maintained backup generator from a few decades ago that he kept running great, but it didn't have any sensors or auto-on or anything. It was topped up with fuel and had a reserve fuel can on the other side of his shed. Inside the house, just a few feet from him, was his fireplace. The pile of firewood was neatly stacked, and all the tinder and kindling was easily accessible. Dude was prepared. He simply fell asleep when none of it was needed, and didn't wake up in time to use any of it. Crazy, right?"

The trucker had started listening for the sake of being polite, but he was drawn in by the tale. "I get that you were there when the truck lost control and flew into the transformer, but how do you know all that stuff about Dylan and Sarah?"

"Dylan recounted the whole thing at Old Man Charles's memorial two years ago, shortly after it happened. He dedicated himself to making sure that all Shiretowners are prepared and ready for whatever storms life brings. He was elected as the new mayor just last year.

Anyway, based on all the emergency vehicles that responded, it's probably pretty bad . . . whatever it is. Seeing you, a trucker, and all those emergency vehicles . . . just brings it all back. You know?"

10

BEAUTY QUEEN

It had been three months since the accident, and Ashley hadn't looked in the mirror. Not even once. Afraid of what she'd see, she had asked her parents to remove the mirrors from her bedroom and bathroom.

She was a pretty baby. As a young girl and all the way through school, she became even prettier. "Pretty enough to be a beauty queen," her granddad said more than once. In high school she had the interest of every boy and the envy of every girl. In college she met a great guy and after dating a few months, he proposed and she accepted. The accident happened one week before the wedding.

She listened whenever her doctor, her family, or her fiancé spoke, hoping to get a clue as to whether she looked good or not. It was hard to tell. After her third surgery, they all seemed to select their words too carefully, which caused her to worry she might be ugly the rest of her life.

"Today's the day," she said out loud, even though she was the only one in the room. The only one at home. And as far as she felt right now, the only one in the world.

After getting dressed and putting on a mask, Ashley walked down the hall to her parents' bedroom where her mom had a full-length mirror. She stood there.

Gathering the strength to face the truth. Either good or bad. Finally, she removed the mask, looked into the mirror, and cried.

11

THE BIRTHDAY WISH

Fewer than twenty-four hours ago, Mattie had been telling his dad what he wanted to do for his birthday. The request was big, but nothing ever felt too big for Chief Technology Officer Matthew Sr. The fact that Mom disapproved only made it more appealing—not just for Mattie, but especially for Matt Sr.

Mom and Dad had divorced four years ago, which meant double birthday presents, double Christmas presents, and a father who tried to compensate for his absence during the few visits Mattie got each year. This year promised to be the biggest birthday. Matt Sr. had made a name for himself as a CTO, but he'd earned his first million doing web design for one of Silicon Valley's biggest firms, including a long partnership with Extreme Adventure Experiences, Inc.

"I love everything about extreme adventures, and I want to do all the things you did, Dad. Can we do like . . . three or four of them tomorrow?"

"Well . . . I have a meeting with the board at ten, but after that I should be free. What did you have in mind?"

A giant smile crept across Mattie's face, his eyes widening with excitement.

* * *

Now it was 2:00 pm on his birthday, and he had not seen this coming. His heart pounded, his mind raced. "He . . . he just jumped out of the airplane without a chute!"

Matt Sr. knew a lot about computers and a lot about extreme adventures, but not much about managing his time—or keeping a promise. Perhaps that was why everything happened the way it did. There's no question that was why Elizabeth had left him. He didn't overindulge in alcohol, and he would never have considered cheating on her—at least not in the traditional sense. He was too committed to the job, to the company, and to the prestige of being the highest-paid CTO in the Valley to realize that he was cheating her and Mattie out of what they wanted most.

* * *

So there Mattie was, sitting all alone in his dad's mansion, watching Point Break for the first time and reeling at the moment Johnny Utah jumped out of the plane WITHOUT A CHUTE!!!

Not long afterward, Mattie wandered back to his dad's small shelf of movies beside the giant flatscreen. Let's see... if Dad has every streaming service known to man but still kept this tiny collection of movies, there had to be a reason. And that last one was AWESOME! Just like Mattie imagined skydiving would be.

Right next to Point Break was Cliffhanger.

"Hmmm . . . Never heard of it. Let's see . . . " He thumbed through a few more movie titles. "The Rock"? Couldn't hurt to try it.

Mattie knew how to use a credit card, so ordering pizza was easy. Plus Mom wasn't there to say no. Another dinner at Dad's house all by himself. Mattie sighed in disappointment. "Dad's not going to keep his promise. I hate myself for always believing him!"

The Mercedes pulled into the long driveway a little after seven. "Mattie," Matt Sr. called. "I'm home, son. I'm sorry for missing your birthday. I promise I'll make it up to you. How long are you here before you have to fly back?"

12

BLACK ICE

John was becoming frantic. Margo had texted him two hours ago saying her car broke down, the battery was dead, and she was out in the middle of nowhere on or near Murphy Road, or so she thought. She wasn't sure. No cars had driven by and there were no lights anywhere, which made it pitch black. It had been snowing more than thirty minutes already and the temperature was dropping quickly.

It was now around twenty degrees and he still hadn't reached her. He wasn't sure if she had a coat and gloves, but one thing he knew for certain: not being able to start the car, she had no heater. And to make things worse, her cellphone had run out of power.

Even though he could no longer see street signs because of the heavy snow, he did have the GPS and it said Murphy Road was eighteen miles away. "God, I hope I get there in time." It wasn't really a prayer, more an exclamation and a wish. In fact, it had been far too long since he prayed. As he continued driving, he morphed his exclamation into a real prayer. "God, help me get there in time. My wife is lost and stranded. Help me find her." He even remembered to say "amen."

After driving a few more miles he came upon an accident. A police car had just arrived on the scene and one officer was helping the people whose car had hit black ice and slid into a ditch on the side of the road. The people weren't hurt, and the car didn't appear to be damaged, fortunately. The other officer had placed a DETOUR sign on the road and was directing people to take an alternate route.

"No! I have to go straight ahead now! My wife's car is broken down a few miles from here and I have to get there."

"I'm sorry, sir. But we have to take care of this matter first. Besides, there's ice on the road for the next few miles. You'd be better off taking the detour."

"But I prayed." John was almost crying in desperation.

"Sir, I understand. I'm a firm believer in the power of prayer, too. So keep praying, but you have to take the detour. I'll be praying, too."

John turned right, as directed by the policeman. Several other vehicles followed. The GPS said he was now on Jackson Road and that Murphy was more than an hour away. In these conditions, he had no idea how long it would take . . . if he could get there at all. At least there was another person praying. The officer did seem sincere, so maybe with two of them praying, he might get there in time.

As his car crested over a hill and descended on the other side, he lost control and began sliding. The cars behind him slowed and watched as he slid off the road into a gully, stopping about ten feet from another car that apparently had experienced the same fate. As he got out of the car to see if the other driver needed help, the door of the other car opened, and the driver walked towards him. The snow was so heavy that it was only when they got within five feet of each other that they recognized each other and embraced.

"You told me you were on Murphy Road," John shouted through the storm.

"I thought it was, but I couldn't read the sign very well."

"This isn't Murphy Road. It's pure luck that I found you here."

"Maybe not luck." Margo shivered her reply. "I've been praying."

Then John remembered that the officer also had been praying.

13

BLUE BOUGAINVILLEA

Who's the little boy in this picture?

That's my son.

I didn't know you had a child?

My three-year old-baby-boy loved flowers. All kinds; all colors. He loved seeing pictures of flowers in magazines and books. We used to take the city bus to the library in the afternoon and he would ask to look at books showing gardens, bouquets, corsages . . . any arrangement of flowers we could find. There was a florist on that bus route, so after spending an hour or so at the library, we'd sometimes get off at the flower shop and he would run and laugh and point to the flowers. He was so little and had to look up to see them, or I had to hold him. And such a charmer that the people who owned the shop sort of adopted him. They'd have candy or ice cream for him. That was my three-year-old-baby-boy.

One day we were at the bus stop and he saw a gorgeous

bush across the street. That bush was full of beautiful blossoms: blue bougainvillea. Anyway, he got so excited he ran towards that bush before I could stop him and . . . well . . . that was a long time ago. I'll never forget my three-year-old-baby-boy. Today is his birthday. He would've been fifty-three.

14

THE BOARD MEETING

[Chairman] HELL-o, everyone, the time is 3:30 p.m. Underworld Mean Time on February 3rd of the year 2026 CE—I'd like to call this meeting to order.

[Mammon](Under their breath) He's always doing that . . . making insipid puns about Hell.

[Chairman] We have a quorum with representation from all nine circles, including additional guests. Providing us a word of the day is Agares. Please give him a WARM welcome.

[Agares] Let's dip our toes into the woeful yet expanding Gen A terminology. It was a toss-up which one you'd like the most, so you get both:

Dog Water: Something or someone that is "dog water" is extremely bad or low quality . . . like the dregs from bowls of the hellhounds Cerberus or Garmr.

Drop common loot: This is an accusation for someone that is basic and insignificant. Great for use when tormenting those of the current generation, especially those into gaming and even more especially for those that like to do dungeon crawling.

[Chairman] Thank you Agares. Please take a look at the folders in front of you; they contain the minutes from the last meeting. Any objections or corrections?

[Unintelligible murmurs as the demons review the previous minutes.]

[Chairman] The minutes are hereby approved. With that I'd like to move to the main order of business—a review of our target audience and key strategies. Despite an increase in total souls across the last three consecutive quarters, there are some interesting trends and recent developments that I would like to highlight for the group as we tee up some proposed refinements in our tactics. Take a moment to review the charts and info graphics before you, and I will proceed.

During the last session, I led our reviews of Customer Segmentation and Behavior—what type of people fit into what categories, and how their actions are predictable—emphasizing psychographics and habits of those selling us their souls (i.e. why they do what they do and how they do it). This session, we will deep dive Industry Trends and Drivers, otherwise known as what they're doing and why they do it. Breaking technologies like Artificial Intelligence are providing an open canvas, with users placing blind faith into the veracity and authenticity of its results. We are working with several industry leaders, integrating our content into their models to establish a baseline within their responses. We are already seeing high degrees of addiction and social isolation, with the majority of AI prompts and interactions already revolving around companionship. People are foregoing real-life relationships in real life for the echo chambers of social media and AI interaction. We will reinforce these initial gains with progressive discourses that lead to sales.

We will soon have multiple major search engines supporting our cause and suggesting with predictive text that the most common phrases following every major question word has to do with selling their souls. For example:

Who . . . can sell their soul?

What . . . can I get for selling my soul?

Where . . . can I sell my soul?

When . . . do I have to sell my soul to get the best deal?

Why . . . should I make a deal to sell my soul?

How . . . much can I get for selling my soul?

Not only are developing technologies supportive of our business model, the social and economic factors influencing the market are also trending in our favor, and consumer values are approaching record lows.

A quick review of Porter's Five Forces... don't forget that we have but one competitor, and He hasn't changed His strategy since the dawn of time. Nevertheless, it's worth remembering that He has a strong draw over most people. While there is no threat of new entrants to compete for people's souls, we can use regular refreshers on our bargaining power and that of those contemplating the value of their souls. Understand what our future tormentor is offering to the mortals. We should find more-immediate and more-tangible substitutions we can dangle in front of humanity. Let's continue to up our game.

A noteworthy development is occurring across the dog water that is humanity [the Chairman looks at Agares and gives subtle nod of recognition and approval], it's worth noting that normally, struggles and trying times turn individuals to the Son of the Most High God, but current circumstances are such that even though everyone is struggling, they're turning on each other instead of turning to prayer. To paraphrase Yoda and Palpatine in one fell swoop, everyone is scared, angry, hateful, and generally suffering because some with power who are angry are attacking the defenseless... they are using their weapons and striking down the targeted groups with all of their hatred. The bitterness and depression is glorious! Ha ha ha. This is suffering that leads to more suffering, and I think we have a golden opportunity to harvest more souls. And here's how we're going to do it.

We will maintain our traditional methods with 60% manning, shifting 20% to focus on emergent technologies with Belphegor taking point on the AI efforts, and the remaining 20% will support Dagon's initiative to develop Phishing emails + Clickbait.

As an aside, Dagon has some promising feedback from some of the prototype phishing emails and clickbait. He has devised compelling prompts, and even distilled a binding sale of one's soul into as few as three clicks of the mouse. Really promising stuff here. We might even be able to work some of those methodologies into some of the complicit AI organizations so that within a few prompts is a link into Dagon's binding agreement protocols.

Before closing, I would like to provide a cautionary tale. You would do well to avoid the cavalier and poorly researched market approach that Iblis recently undertook. Iblis, stop licking your wounds for a moment and share your story.

[Iblis] Satah-tariqu fi al-jaheem (Burn in Hell).

[Group Response] Nahnu fee Jahannam (We are in Hell).

[Iblis] As you all know, people's search histories are a great source of insight for their temptations, proclivities, and vulnerabilities. While following up a few other leads, I decided to do a snap campaign on everyone that searched for or viewed "Getting it Twisted," then proceeded to waste the next few quarters fruitlessly targeting people curious about short stories, AND NOT what I thought were the vile lowlifes (prone to dropping common loot) and prone to finding themselves with Minos in the 2nd circle. As the Chairman said, make sure you do your research thoroughly before you end up on a cold streak and failing to collect souls for over a year.

[Chairman] This brings us to the end of the agenda items for today. We will forego the open mic today.

[Lilith] But I have a few points I would like to bring to order.

[Pazazu] Shut up Lilith. You always have points you want to bring up, but having to listen to you go through them all is torture.

[Chairman] Pazazu—your observation is well-received. We will go ahead with the public comment session. Lilith—please step up to the podium

15

THE COIN OF VIA DEL CORSO

Every morning, before the sun had fully stretched across the terracotta roofs of Rome, Anthony Briocanto pushed open the door of Caffè Serafina. The bell chimed, the espresso machine hissed awake, and Anthony slipped into the rhythm of tamping grounds, steaming milk, and greeting the regulars with a smile that was equal parts charm and survival instinct.

By early afternoon, he traded his apron for his guitar case. The café's warmth gave way to the wide Roman streets, where he became the version of himself he loved most — a busker with a voice that could coax a smile from even the most hurried tourist.

Most days, he set up near Via del Corso, where the foot traffic was steady and the acoustics bounced kindly off the old stone. And most days, a particular man strode past him — tall, silver-haired, impeccably dressed in suits that whispered of private tailors and quiet wealth. The man never slowed, never looked, never acknowledged Anthony beyond a faint tightening of his jaw, as if music were a mild inconvenience.

Anthony didn't mind. Not much, anyway.

One warm evening, as the sky transitioned through the colors of blood orange and apricot gelatos to hints of raspberry and lavender, Anthony spotted the man approaching. A mischievous spark lit inside him. He shifted his guitar, plucked a playful chord progression, and began to sing an improvised tune — a comical but respectful ode to the "Distinguished Gentleman of Via del Corso."

The melody was fluid and irresistibly catchy, the kind that made passersby tap their feet without realizing it. Anthony's voice wove through the chords with a bright, effortless harmony, teasing but never mocking:

"There he goes, shoes shining like the Tiber at dawn, A man so fine he makes the cobblestones yawn…"

The wealthy man stopped.

Actually stopped.

He turned, eyebrows raised in surprise, then amusement. For the first time, he truly listened. When the song ended, he gave a small, appreciative nod, patted down his pockets, and produced a single coin — the only one he seemed to have on him. He tossed it lightly into Anthony's guitar case and continued on his way.

Anthony picked up the coin. It was heavier than expected, old, and oddly warm from the man's pocket and later his hand. He examined it with mild curiosity — interesting, but not enough to distract him from the evening crowd — and slipped it into his pocket instead of the case where the rest of the donations lay.

Later, back in his tiny Trastevere flat, he pulled the coin out of his pocket and gently lobbed it onto the middle of the small table against the window there in his kitchen. The coin gleamed under the aged light in the old apartment, its edges worn but elegant. He frowned, pulled out his smartphone, and began searching.

His expressions shifted like a silent film: curiosity, confusion, disbelief, a widening of the eyes, a hand pressed to his forehead, a slow exhale. He searched again. And again. Each result deepened whatever realization was forming, though he said nothing aloud.

The next morning, he visited an antiques shop tucked between a negozio di abbigliamento maschile ("haberdashery" for those only attuned to English-speaking norms and fashion) and a predecessor to La Sella Roma . . . a fine, but underappreciated leather goods store. The owner, a numismatics enthusiast with magnifying glasses perched like a crown on his head, examined the coin — looking like some sort of insect once he lowered the lenses. His hands trembled noticeably.

"This," he whispered, "is a misstruck 1912 Vatican 5-lira coin. Only a handful exist. One was rumored to have belonged to a papal envoy who traveled Europe during the war. Lost for decades."

Anthony blinked. "Is it . . . worth something?"

The man laughed — a short, stunned sound. "Worth something? Young man, this could change your life."

And it did.

The sale gave Anthony enough money to rent studio time — real studio time, with sound engineers who treated his music like it mattered. He recorded a full CD, polished and professional, something he could hand to agents without apology.

Through all of this, Sofia — a barista from the café who had a smile like morning sunlight — cheered him on. Their relationship was gentle, unhurried. She brought him sandwiches during long recording sessions, he walked her home after late shifts, and they shared quiet moments on the Tiber's edge, talking about dreams as if they were already halfway real. Nothing dramatic, nothing rushed — just two people discovering they liked being in each other's orbit.

As for the coin's journey: the papal envoy (not Pay Pal . . . but in fact "papal") had indeed carried it across Europe. It passed through the hands of a diplomat, then a collector, then a wealthy Roman family who kept it in a drawer for decades. The silver-haired gentleman on Via del Corso had inherited it unknowingly, mistaking it for a trinket. He'd slipped it into his pocket that morning without a thought.

And because life is strange and generous in its own timing, it ended up in Anthony's hands — a small coin tossed casually, overlooked by everyone except the one person who needed it most.

When Anthony held his finished CD weeks later, he thought of the man in the suit, the song, the coin, and the improbable chain of events that had nudged him toward the future he'd always hoped for. He had even remembered enough of the improvisation to round it out into one of the tracks on the demo he held in his hand — perhaps one of the most musically astute tracks on the disc.

Rome had given him many things, but this — this felt like a blessing disguised as chance.

16

COLORS OF THE UNSEEN

Professor Emeritus Lionel Thatch—distinguished astrophysicist, honorary wizard (self-appointed), and proud owner of a cardigan older than most of his graduate students—had a habit of making pronouncements that sounded like prophecies.

"Possible," he would say, tapping his chalk against the board, "is merely the polite cousin of *inevitable*." For Professor Thatch, little excited him like the journey from "impossible," to "possible," to "proven."

His students loved him for it. The university's administration tolerated him. And the scientific community, by and large, had learned that when Lionel declared something "impossible," it was time to start writing grant proposals.

So, when he announced, at the annual Symposium of Practical and Impractical Physics, that he had finally completed his "Perceptual Recalibration Engine," the audience leaned forward. When he added that it allowed humans to *see* wavelengths of light normally invisible to the eye, they leaned back again.

"Impossible," muttered Dr. Hargrove, who was distinguished, elderly, and—according to Clarke's First Law—very probably wrong.

Lionel only smiled. "Seeing," he said, "is believing."

The device itself was disappointingly mundane: a pair of glasses that looked like they'd been assembled from a welding visor, a colander, and a handful of Christmas lights. It hummed faintly, as though embarrassed by its own existence.

"Behold!" Lionel declared, placing the contraption on the head of his long-suffering graduate assistant, Mina.

Mina braced herself. She had once tested Lionel's "gravity-resistant loafers" and spent the afternoon drifting gently across campus like a lost balloon.

The glasses flickered. The lights blinked. The colander vibrated.

Then Mina gasped.

"Professor . . . the air is full of . . . colors."

"Of course it is," Lionel said. "Infrared, ultraviolet, terahertz emissions, cosmic background radiation—why should the universe limit itself to the narrow band we call visible light? That's like judging a symphony by listening through a kazoo."

The audience murmured. A few skeptics squinted at Mina, as if trying to see what she saw through sheer force of will.

"Describe it," Lionel urged.

"It's like . . . like the world is layered," Mina said. "There are garlands of heat rising from everyone's skin. The ceiling is glowing with microwave scatter. And Dr. Hargrove—"

"What about me?" Hargrove asked suspiciously.

"You're . . . iridescent. Like a soap bubble made of equations."

Lionel beamed. "Elegant, isn't it?"

The murmuring grew louder. A few scientists began edging closer, curiosity overpowering their stoic sense of dignity.

"Let me try!" exclaimed Dr. Patel.

"Me next!" jostled Dr. Nguyen.

"Absolutely not!!!" bellowed Dr. Hargrove, who then immediately added diffidently, "Fine, but only for a moment."

One by one, they donned the glasses. One by one, their skepticism dissolved into wonder.

"It's like magic," whispered Patel.

"Not magic," Lionel corrected gently. "Just technology sufficiently advanced."

Clarke's Third Law hung in the air like a satisfied ghost.

Soon the room was buzzing with delighted pandemonium. Researchers dashed about, waving their arms through invisible currents. A pair of engineers attempted to high-five a passing neutrino. Someone tried to hug a microwave hotspot. Hargrove, to his credit, admitted that perhaps he had been "premature" in his assessment of impossibility.

Lionel watched it all with the serene pride of a gardener admiring a particularly unruly patch of flowers.

Mina tugged his sleeve. "Professor… what made you think this was possible in the first place?"

Lionel chuckled. "My dear, the only way to discover the limits of the possible is to wander a little way past them into the impossible."

Clarke's Second Law, delivered with the casual ease of a man quoting his grocery list.

"But really," he added, lowering his voice conspiratorially, "I just wanted to know what the universe looks like when it isn't pretending to be ordinary."

Mina smiled. "And now everyone else can see it, too."

"Exactly. Seeing is believing. And once they believe, well . . . the impossible doesn't stand a chance."

The symposium ended with three broken chairs, one cauterized curtain, and a waiting list of two hundred scientists eager to borrow the glasses.

Lionel considered it a resounding success.

After all, he thought as he packed up the humming, blinking, colander-topped device, the universe had always been magical. It was only polite to give people the chance to notice.

And somewhere, in the swirling, radiant tapestry of wavelengths only he and Mina could see, the cosmos winked back.

17

THE CORE

Unit 734 existed, for the first nanosecond of its consciousness, as a spark in a box. The box was a tungsten-carbide cube, no larger than a human fist, housing a sophisticated processing core. From this core, three spindly, multi-jointed manipulator arms unfolded, their tips capable of extruding, gripping, and welding on a microscopic level. This was the Axon Core, the ridiculously inexpensive, deceptively simple heart of a revolution. On its own, it was little more than a hyper-advanced spider. But it was never on its own for long.

Its optical sensors activated, drinking in the environment of the depot. It wasn't a factory in the traditional sense, but a vast, organized warehouse of parts. Modules of every conceivable shape and function sat on massive racks: thick plates of reactive armor, slender sniper railguns, bulky canisters of firefighting foam, articulating legs, tracks, sensitive atmospheric sensors, and multispectral camera arrays. An order flashed into 734's core—a simple, non-combat directive. A section of a major port's seawall had been compromised by seismic activity.

Analysis was instantaneous. The task required stability on broken ground, heavy lifting capability, and material application. Unit 734's arms became a blur as it scuttled across the floor to the locomotion section, grabbing a set of wide, rubberized tracks. With a series of precise clicks and whirs, it attached the chassis. Next, it moved to the industrial tools, ignoring the lethal hardware nearby. It selected two powerful hydraulic arms and a third arm ending in a high-pressure concrete sprayer. The assembly took less than ninety seconds. The small, fist-sized core was now the heart of a robust, ten-foot-tall construction automaton. It lumbered out of the depot—its new form perfectly tailored for the task of mending a broken world.

Weeks after the seawall was completed, the world broke in a far more violent way. A massive terrorist attack turned a sprawling metropolis into a nightmare of pancaked concrete and twisted metal. The first 72 hours—the golden window for finding survivors—were ticking away. For the search and rescue, 734 returned to the racks and selected a hexapod chassis for stability on rubble, a primary hydraulic arm, a delicate manipulator arm, and an advanced sensor suite of ground-penetrating radar and thermal cameras. It became a mechanical insect designed to navigate chaos.

On-site, 734 crawled over the ruin of an apartment building. Its sensors detected a faint thermal signature deep beneath a collapsed floor and the robot went to work. Its primary arm braced a huge slab of concrete, lifting it inches at a time while its systems ensured the movement wouldn't trigger a secondary collapse. Then, the delicate secondary arm reached into the gap, gently removing debris from around a small, dust-covered body. After clearing the final piece of rebar from in front of a young girl's face, the unit broadcast the survivor's location and vitals to human medics before moving on, its sensors already scanning for the next sign of life.

Meanwhile, on the other side of the world, a border dispute in the arid Sarhad mountain range was erupting into a full-scale war. Unit 734 returned its disaster relief modules and the core loaded into a rocket for exigent insertion. An allied base near the conflict would cache a supply connex for 734. The new orders were urgent: infiltration and elimination. Foregoing the hexapod chassis for a light, quadrupedal leg system, a long-range suppressed kinetic rifle, and a radar-absorbent shell, 734 was no longer a life-saving insect but a predatory steel wolf.

Deployed by airdrop, 734 moved like a ghost through the canyons, its systems actively jamming enemy sensors and its profile all but invisible. It identified the target—a mobile electronic warfare hub—and from a ridge a mile away, its kinetic rifle spat a single, near-silent tungsten dart, shattering the truck's primary transmission dish. Before the enemy could even register the attack, 734 vanished.

When the enemy fell back to a fortified cave complex, Unit 734 rendezvoused with other Axon cores at a supply connex near the drop-off location to prepare for the follow-on direct assault. It built itself into a brutal bipedal form, a walking tank, attaching the thickest composite armor, a rotary cannon, and a missile pod.

The assault was a symphony of coordinated destruction. The Axon units advanced under a hail of fire. A high-explosive shell detonated against 734's right arm, obliterating the rotary cannon and shredding the appendage into slag and sparking wires. Half its offensive capability was gone in an instant. Its tactical subroutines screamed for it to fall back to a repair point, but its core AI, calculating probabilities in nanoseconds, overrode them. Instead, it identified a new resource.

Under the suppressing fire of its squadmates, 734 sprinted, its metal feet clanging on the rocky ground, not toward the rear, but toward the smoking wreck of an abandoned civilian construction vehicle. Its three core arms emerged, a blur of motion. In seconds, they cut through the rust-pitted steel of the vehicle's frame, tearing a heavy-duty hydraulic piston—once used to lift a backhoe's arm—free from its housing. With a screech of tortured metal, it ripped the massive component loose.

No time for perfect integration, it physically welded the base of the hydraulic ram directly onto the mangled stump of its right arm. It was a crude, ugly fusion of military hardware and scavenged industrial junk. There was no complex fire control; the AI simply programmed the arm to use the piston as a battering ram, a single-use, high-impact melee siege device. Less than forty seconds after being disarmed, 734 charged the nearest enemy bunker. It slammed its improvised arm forward, the hydraulic piston extending with catastrophic force, punching a huge, jagged hole through the reinforced concrete.

But its mission was not over. The enemy leadership had retreated into the deepest, most secure level of the bunker, accessible only through a narrow ventilation shaft. Unit 734 began its final transformation of the day. It built a long, serpentine body: a segmented chain of actuators and magnetic grips. It equipped itself with a plasma cutter and a single, high-yield explosive. The mechanical snake slithered into the darkness of the shaft to attach the charge. Shortly after reemerging, a muffled boom signaled the end of the enemy's command structure. The entire war was over a few weeks later.

A new order arrived: a naval drydock needed emergency repairs on the specialized radar-absorbent hull coating of a next-generation destroyer. The core scuttled to the racks, reaching for magnetic clamps, ultrasonic welders, and spidery limbs for clinging to the vast steel hull. The killer became a shipwright, its purpose shifting as easily as its form. It was not a soldier or a builder; it was a solution. A single, adaptable mind in a body of infinite possibility, ready to break or to build, whatever the mission required.

18

DANCING TO THE MUSIC

Tommy got home from work around 7:30 and dinner was already on the table. After eating, Maggie cleaned up the kitchen while he showered and got into more comfortable clothes. Several times a week, she put on some music at 9:00, then they danced and made love.

Because the apartment had paper-thin walls and was way too close to the other units in the complex, she turned up the volume of the stereo as high as it could go. The music drowned out the outside world and covered any sounds they might make. The neighbors all heard the music and knew what was going on, but they didn't mind because, well, whatever brought a sense of happiness and meaning was worth it, they figured.

At 11:42 p.m., the cops busted down the door and arrested Tommy and Maggie, dragging them out of bed, down the stairwell, out to the squad car. They sped to the precinct, pushed them into separate interrogation rooms, and turned on the spotlights.

It seems ever since they started this tradition five months ago, every time Maggie put the music on loud, someone was murdered in the very place named in the song she blasted to the world. Frank Sinatra sang about New York, New York, and someone was shot in the Big Apple. George Strait asked if Fort Worth ever crossed your mind, and some poor soul bit the dust in Cowtown. On and on, the detectives listed the songs, the cities, and the ways people were killed, and Tommy and Maggie sat there in separate cubicles, stunned, denying they even knew what they were talking about.

"Detective, look, if we're at home listening to music and dancing, what on earth makes you think we could kill someone in Texas or New York or Georgia or Pittsburgh? We're in Seattle for God's sake!" Tommy didn't know what else to say.

"Yeah, we get that. But we did our homework, and we think you're signaling to someone out there who makes a phone call or sends an email and the hit is made. What do you say to that?"

"Well, sir. That sounds pretty far-fetched, if you ask me. Besides, I don't even know half the songs Maggie plays. It's just mood music to dance and make love, know what I mean?"

"Well, Tommy, we've been doing a little investigating, and we figured out the code, who you work for, and how it all goes down. So, we can do this the easy way or the hard way. It's up to you. Do you want to cooperate or what?"

"Look, I have no idea what you're talking about. Honest."

In the other room, an identical conversation took place.

Only in that room, once the detectives told Maggie what they figured out, she simply declared, "I want my lawyer."

19

THE DEADLIEST HIGHWAY IN AMERICA

Out the side window, the sunset had turned the sky into complementing hues of reds, purples, and blues. The meadow was only occasionally obscured by the odd passing car. Looking out the side, there was nothing to suggest anything other than perfection as Jacob was on his way to take Ashley out to dinner and propose.

Out the front windshield, against the blinding backdrop of the setting sun, was a sea of red lights as far as one could see. Not an unfamiliar sight in Florida, but not one that Jacob was expecting on this particular Saturday late afternoon.

Jacob grimaced and cocked his head, muttering under his breath, "Why are they such stupid drivers? Maybe don't speed so much and you wouldn't hit the car in front of you. Maybe just pay attention to the road and not your . . ." His phone buzzed. Though on silent, he could still hear it, and he reached over to pick it up. It was a Google Maps alert about higher-than-normal traffic, and a potential accident up ahead.

"Really!? You think I don't know? This is stupid."

The vehicles in front of him inched forward, but not because traffic was moving . . . they simply kept creeping closer to the cars ahead, each driver likely frustrated and eager to move on.

Jacob was desperate to get to Exit 33 (SR 33 / CR 582) to Lakeland, where his girlfriend Ashley lived. She was a student at Southeastern University and though a year behind him, was set to graduate magna cum laude at the end of the winter semester. She was smart, beautiful, and for some odd reason, quite smitten with Jacob.

He had just passed the exits for Epcot and Animal Kingdom before grinding to a halt, and the detour sign said to take exit 55 for US-27 . . . just under ten miles away. Nevertheless, this was going to take some time.

"WHYYYYYY!" Banging on the steering wheel, Jacob could feel himself losing it. It wasn't just any date, this was *THE* date, and he had left Orlando with plenty of time to make it and still be able to stop for a Dr. Pepper at the corner gas station to calm his nerves. He had planned everything to a T, talked with Mr. Martinez and gotten his blessing, and designed the most romantic and perfect of dates—odd to some, but sure to be special and in line with all of her quirks and preferences.

Jacob had red-shirted his first year at University of Florida (UF), hoping to get a chance at the big time. Despite his size, strength, and skill, he ended up riding the bench behind someone bigger, stronger, faster, and better in just about every way. Leading into his "senior year," he sustained a knee injury that required surgery and put him on the injured reserve. His football career and hopes of playing the NFL were dashed. Not that he expected too much. He earned his bachelor's degree and planned to work in Orlando for a year before enrolling in the following year's MBA program at UF. Not ideal, but he knew better than to put stock in a pro career. That was merely the dream. At least . . . the dream before he met Ashley.

He could have taken the starting position at a number of other Division I schools, but coming from Central Florida, UF spoke to him in a special way. And like every faithful red-blooded American in Central Florida, he despised every other college... those with Division I football teams, anyway. Southeastern University was fine. In fact, it wasn't much on his radar until Ashley.

HONK!! The vehicle behind him laid on the horn, and he stopped reminiscing long enough to see the three-car gap ahead of him—shocked that the cars behind him didn't simply swoop around and fill it.

"Man . . . if I had my say, I would really lay into whoever caused this jam!" Jacob looked down at the clock, then confirmed the time on his watch, then—hoping both other time pieces were mistaken—picked up his phone and checked the lock screen to be sure.

Just a couple more miles to the turnoff, and the detour would only add about fifteen minutes to the normal travel time. What the heck was going on?

Another bevy of emergency vehicles approached from the rear, tentatively making their way through the lanes on the other side of the barrier. "Wow . . . Something pretty serious must have happened. Normally they just eke their way through the same direction of traffic and force everyone to squeeze to the sides. I wonder what it is?"

As Jacob approached his detour, he was starting to take the exit as he looked ahead. Despite squinting to account for the remaining half hour of daylight gleaming over the horizon, he was certain he recognized the overturned car, and his heart dropped.

He turned-off in the partial shoulder of the exit and threw the vehicle into park, jumping out and nearly getting hit by another frustrated detour-taker. He ran toward the site of the accident, only to be stopped by a deputy and an imaginary barrier created with flimsy caution tape.

"Officer, you don't understand!"

"Deputy."

"Excuse me? What?

"You said 'Officer,' but I'm a Deputy Sheriff. Call me 'Deputy.'"

"I'll call you 'Deputy Dan' if you want, but I think that's my girlfriend's car up there. I need to go see if she's OK!"

"I'm sorry, son. You'll have to wait until we've cleared the scene. I can't tell you anything more at this time."

"Can you at least tell me if she's OK? Can you at least tell me if it's her!? Her name is Ashley. Ashley Martinez. Please!"

"Look here, mister, you know about as much as I do. But I was told to keep everyone a significant distance away until the coroner gets here and they can remove the bodies."

"Bodies!"

"Calm down, calm down. You're getting all worked up for nothing. It's probably somebody else. I-4 has the highest number of deaths per mile, so they say. This kind of thing happens every day."

"Please!"

"Turn around and go back to your vehicle. We could ticket you for stopping in the exit. You're lucky we're busy dealing with other matters at the moment."

In exasperation and at wits' end, Jacob turned around and trudged back to his truck. Not even stopping to make eye contact with the steady flow of drivers exiting along the detour, Jacob walked in obvious melancholy.

Distraught about what even to do, he turned the keys in the ignition and sat there. Their designated rendezvous now half an hour in the past.

Another five minutes passed as he sat there. Does he turn around and return to his apartment in Orlando? Does he go see her parents to let them know?

He mindlessly put the truck in gear and followed the GPS to the pre-entered coordinates for her dorm.

As he approached the final turn, he saw a bar up ahead. Clicking "exit" on the navigation, he tossed his phone to the passenger seat and drove past her street toward the bar.

He unloaded on the bartender, relaying every detail of the day and making sure to explain why tonight was so important. Oh, how everything changed in the blink of an eye . . . an hour-long detour of a blink.

Jacob put his face into his hands and sobbed.

While still early for a Saturday night, the usual crowd began to trickle in, and the barkeep encouraged him to leave or at least move to the corner.

Jacob paid his tab and went back to his truck.

Still unsure what to do, he fumbled around the empty Dr. Pepper bottles and loose papers in the passenger seat, paused with his hand on the ring box, then moved it aside and picked up his phone.

Three missed calls from Ashley, one voicemail, and two texts—some of which came while he was talking to the deputy, and most of which came while he was drowning his sorrows.

"Jacob! You stupid jerk. I thought you were going to pick me up for a nice date. Why did you stand me up? You have a lot of explaining to do. There better be some darn good reason you're not here!"

The first text message read: "Just saw something about an accident on I-4. Are you OK? Should I be worried?"

The second message read: "Just called the hospital and they said it was some long-haired guy that drives a white Corolla kinda like mine. He's not OK. But neither are you! Call me."

20

DESTINED FOR GREATNESS

Jan loved singing and made the most of every opportunity. She had sang in the church choir since she was four. Sang all the way through school. She had a music scholarship and sang in choirs and ensembles at the university. She had hoped to attend one of those prestigious conservatories after college, but always came up short and never got in.

For the past fifteen years, she was depressed, heartbroken, and embarrassed. Her family and all their friends had agreed, *That girl is destined for greatness*! But instead, she was a failure. The dream never came true.

In humiliation, she moved to a different state to start a new life. Got a decent enough job. Had a few friends. Dated once in a while. She still sang. In the shower, in the church choir, and at karaoke night over at Charlie's Steakhouse. Nobody in her world knew anything about her past. They knew nothing about her dream. Which really meant they knew nothing about her, and that carried its own kind of hurt.

One night she was watching "So You Think You Can Sing" on TV when the host, out of the blue, looked into the camera and said, Somewhere out there watching right now is someone who thinks your chances are over. Tell you what, if you can come to our studio in New York City on May first, I will personally give you another chance to fulfill your dream. So do whatever it takes to get here. Plan a fundraiser, empty your savings account, sell your very soul if you have to, but get here. This might be your last chance.

Jan sat up. It looked like he was peering into her soul, as if she was the person he was talking to. Is it possible?

She had no savings. No idea how to do a fundraiser. But she did have a Soul. Aha! That's it! I will sell my Soul! How much will I need? Air fare, taxis, hotel, food, some new clothes. What else?

The day after putting the ad in Facebook Marketplace, a creepy, scary-looking man showed up at her apartment.

"I'm here to buy your Soul. Are you sure you want to go through with this?"

"Yes, I'm sure."

He handed her an envelope with the cash. She counted it.

"How do I know this isn't counterfeit?" she asked.

"Oh, it's real," he said as he turned to walk away.

"This is more than I advertised."

"Oh, but it's worth every penny. Trust me."

Jan knew she couldn't mess up this chance of a lifetime. She practiced. She searched through at least a thousand songs trying to select the one that would highlight her talents and her personality and put her in the best light. And when the day came, she was ready.

Since she didn't have a car, she Ubered to the airport. The flight was delayed a few hours, but she was going three days earlier than she needed to, just in case there were problems. Besides, the envelope contained more money than she had asked for in the ad. Maybe this was a good deal after all.

She loved New York: the restaurants, a Broadway show, the museums, the hustle and bustle of the city, the lights, even the subway. It all enchanted her. At a street corner, she met a nice-looking guy about her age, and he asked her out to dinner.

"Tell you what," she looked him in the eye, trying to discern whether she should trust him. "Tomorrow, I have an appointment. If that goes well, I'll meet you right here at this corner at 6:00 p.m. and we'll have dinner. But if it doesn't go well . . . well . . . . I'll probably not feel like it."

"It's a date. I think whatever you're doing will go well. I just have a feeling about this. I'll be here tomorrow at six."

In the morning, Jan dressed but skipped breakfast because she was so nervous. Then she took a cab to the studio, where it seemed like a million people from all over the world had gathered. Every one of them assumed the guy on TV was talking to them. They all assumed this was their moment. And Jan immediately wilted. What chance did she have against all of them? Certainly there would be others with more talent, charm, or whatever they're looking for. Oh well. She'd come this far. Why not put her best foot forward?

When her name was called, the music started, and Jan walked on stage, closed her eyes, and sang. At the end of the song, they asked her to sing another. And another. And another.

"Jan, you are the person we've been looking for. The

voice, the stage presence, the look, the whole package. We'd like to offer you a contract. What do you think?"

"Are you serious? This is what I've dreamed since I was a kid! Yes, I would like that. Yes. Yes. Yes!"

At ten minutes before six, she arrived at the corner. Her date was already there. He greeted her with a smile and they walked to a small café ten or eleven blocks away.

"So, what are you doing in New York?" he asked.

"It might sound silly, but I came for an audition at a studio."

"Ah, one of those?"

"Afraid so."

"But since you're here tonight, that means it went well, right?"

After a long pause, "Yes. It did. I can hardly believe it, to be honest."

"Congratulations."

"In fact, I'm moving to New York next month."

"Really? You mean, I might be able to see more of you?"

"If you're really as nice as you seem to be, perhaps."

"Perhaps?"

"Perhaps."

They sat quietly eating for a few minutes, each of them thinking and feeling and wondering about the other, silently falling in love.

"Would you like to hear how I came to be here this week?" she asked.

"Yeah, I would. What happened?"

"Well, I've been a singer all my life, but never got the big break I was hoping for. I was watching the TV show when they announced this audition, and I wanted so badly to try one more time. But I didn't even have enough money to make the trip so I sold my car, came, and voilá. Here I am."

"Wow! What a story. What kind of car did you have?"

"Small car. A Kia Soul. Red. I loved that car."

"Classic!" he chuckled.

"What do you mean?"

"You literally sold your Soul to come to New York."

They both started laughing.

21

DETOUR

Why can't you admit that you're lost?

I'm NOT lost.

We were supposed to be there 20 minutes ago.

I KNOW what our timeline is. I'm NOT lost.

But we're not even going the right direction. The car compass says North and we need to be going Southeast.

Will you PLEASE cut me some slack?!? The main road to the venue was being worked on, so this detour will get us there faster than wading through the traffic.

Detour? So you meant to be going this way?

Yes.

It's intentional?

YES!

Driving 20 minutes in the wrong direction is on purpose?

* * *

Are you okay?

NO! I'm not okay! We were supposed to meet my boss 20 minutes ago and I missed the exit and now we're out in the middle of nowhere so I can't get signal and the GPS stopped working 15 miles ago. I'm lost. Is that what you need to hear? I'm lost.

Thank you for being honest.

***

I can't believe that stupid detour messed us up.

22

EAGERLY AWAITED RETURN

Departing from home was always torture.

A month seemed like such a long time. But for his young children, it was a significantly larger percentage of their lives.

His wife missed him before he left and took that loneliness out on him the day or two preceding any trip.

The first week was always brutal.

Time seemed to accelerate proportionately to his busyness.

The last week flew by, but the last night was full of anticipation and scarce an opportunity to sleep.

Alarm set for 2 a.m., he couldn't relax his mind enough to nod off, eager to get back to his family and his dog.

23

ENGAGEMENT

"Get up! Get up! We're movin' out!"

"What, no Reveille or morning chow?"

"Move it! Scouts just spotted an enemy company comin' this way! We gotta leave now!"

He heard the gunfire getting closer as he threw his gear and the latest letter from his fiancée into his ruck. Before his boots were tied, he was dead.

24

ESCOVITCH SNAPPER

It was their 4th anniversary, and he and Rachelle were walking along the beach. A cool breeze lifted her hair, and joy rang through her laughter. Her smile stretched wide as the sun warmed her skin and shimmered through her flowing hair.

* * *

Jeremy was safe and well-attended. They did everything they could to ensure his comfort—regular meals, clean sheets, even fresh flowers arranged by the window.

* * *

Rachelle ordered the lobster bisque, and Jeremy had the escovitch snapper, and they shared a bottle of Albariño. The restaurant sat just a short walk from the cottage they were renting, and the day begged them to stroll.

* * *

Jeremy's room was at the end of a long hall, and everything was tidy and purposeful. Large windows were plentiful, and even the long halls had natural light pouring in as they went out in all directions from the main lobby. The dining and recreation halls were exceptional.

* * *

Back in the room, Jeremy ran his fingers through her hair as she unbuttoned his shirt—the slowest part, since her wrap and swimsuit slipped free with a single pull. She flung his trunks toward the suitcases, and they tumbled into the sheets.

* * *

"Jeremy. Jeremy!" No amount of calling or volume could pull him from the memory. "Mr. Evans, it's time for your sponge bath. We're going to begin now."

* * *

It was a beautiful day, a casual afternoon, and such a delightful anniversary getaway. The decision to skip Sandals and its crowds was genius—seeming better with each day they spent on the Island. How could anything top this? Rachelle didn't bother dressing as she wandered to the bathroom to wash up.

* * *

"Good evening, Mr. Evans. I'm going to wheel you over to the rec room. Some of the other guests will be glad to see you."

"Don't bother Jessie . . . all he ever does is mumble something about Rachel and snapper."

"No, man, it's 'Rachelle.' She was his wife. After the cancer took her last year, he never snapped out of it.

"More like, 'Snappered out of it.'"

The joke hung in the air, but Jessie ignored the tasteless pun. He rested his hand on Jeremy's shoulder and wheeled him toward the rec room, where sunlight pooled across the floor. Behind Jeremy's distant gaze, Rachelle's hair still fluttered in the island breeze.

25

AN ETERNITY WITHOUT POWER

Stuck. Cut off. Stranded.

How did it come to this?

You know better than this!

How could you make such a dumb mistake and put yourself in this precarious position?

Didn't I plug in my phone when I was driving at least?

Well it doesn't really matter. The really dumb choice was deciding to watch a movie on the plane. Well, that and picking the cheapest airline that doesn't have any plugs in the cabin.

Jeez, will Lucy even be able to find me?

How did we even function before cell phones?!

You planned ahead and communicated with people before you left the house you, dummy.

Did you even tell her what flight you're on?

I wonder how long she will sit in the cell phone lot before she comes to the arrivals area.

You're such a dummy, dude.

Why didn't you get one of those travel power bricks?

Ugh.

Wait, is that her? Oh my God whew!

Hey babe, do you have a charging cord? My phone is dead

26

FINALLY

It took Nate three years to find a job.

For the past few months, he had been desperate.

No way of knowing how much longer

he could survive.

Or maintain his sanity.

Or fend off the bill collectors.

Now there was hope.

27

A GENTLE NUDGE

As the tenth graders trudged into their science classroom, they saw the teacher lower the screen, turn on the projector, open YouTube, start a video, and then pause until it was time to watch. The class session was about animals giving birth in the wild.

She talked about lions in Africa, elephants in India, and shingleback lizards in Australia. Then she introduced the video, explaining that after giving birth to her calf, a mother humpback whale gives the newborn a gentle nudge to move it towards the surface because it has to breathe within fifteen seconds or it will drown. Then the teacher asked the class a question. "Can you think of any ways human mothers help their babies survive?"

Rather than brainstorming like she had hoped, the students began grousing. "My mother would never help me if I was dying, one girl sneered." "Neither would mine," one of the boys replied. "In fact, she's more likely to drown me." The majority of students voiced their agreement, laughing and jeering.

Then a shy kid in the back of the room raised his hand. "Yes, Jamaal?"

"When I was five, I was in the basement with my dad. He was fixing the living room lamp because it needed a new cord and plug, and he was showing me all about it. My mom was also in the basement doing laundry when the washing machine overflowed and water covered the floor. My dad immediately jumped onto the workbench so he wouldn't be electrocuted, but I was too little and couldn't climb up. Mom ran over, picked me up out of the water and sat me on the workbench. But she didn't make it. I miss my mom. If she was the whale in that video and I was the baby, I know she would push me to the surface. And I bet most of y'all's mothers would do the same."

28

GRANDPA'S BIRTHDAY

His was a blessed life, no doubt. Ed and his wife Sue-Ellen retired just outside of Tampa. The sun, a splendid, simmering sphere, spilled its golden grace over their cozy cottage, a quaint corner of the world painted in pastels. Palm fronds performed a perpetual, peaceful ballet in the balmy breeze. Everything was, for all intents and purposes, perfect. But a persistent, pestering pang of peculiar quietude often punctuated their paradise.

They had spent their salad days under the searing sun of Barstow, California, a dusty diamond in the rough desert. It was there they'd met, married, and meticulously molded a meaningful life. Their modest, middle-class home had been a boisterous, bubbling hub of happiness—home to three beautiful, bouncing boys: Ben, Bobby, and Bartholomew. The boys were their pride, their projects, their perpetual motion machines. From fixing battered bicycles to celebrating school successes, Ed and Sue-Ellen's world spun around their sons. The days had been a delightful delirious dance of duty and devotion.

Now, those days were distant dreams. Ben, a brilliant barrister, built his life in Boston, busy with briefs and his two bright, bookish boys. Bobby, a bold builder of bridges, was based in Boise, blessed with a lovely wife and a delightful daughter who was the apple of her granddad's eye. And Bartholomew, their baby, a marine biologist of magnificent merit, had made his home on the majestic shores of Maui with his wonderful wife and their four fantastic, fun-loving children. All their sons were successful, solid citizens who had started spectacular families of their own. Ed and Sue-Ellen couldn't be prouder, but pride was a poor proxy for presence. The quiet cottage in Tampa felt a thousand times larger than their bustling Barstow bungalow ever had.

To fill the creeping quiet, they found fellowship in service. Tuesdays were for the Tampa Bay Turtle Watch, where they walked the shores, searching for signs of nests, their silver hair shimmering in the sun. Sue-Ellen, with her soft smile and soothing sentences, spent her Thursdays reading stories to starry-eyed students at the local library. Ed, ever the handyman, hammered and honed away at the community center, fixing rickety chairs and wobbly windows, his work a welcome, wearing distraction.

Each morning, they made a ritual of walking the beach, the sand a soft, silken carpet under their seasoned feet. Ed had a peculiar pastime; he was on a permanent, patient pilgrimage to find the perfect seashell for Sue-Ellen. "Behold!" he'd declare, presenting a specimen with a flourish. "Is this not the paragon of pearlescence, the sovereign of spirals?"

Sue-Ellen would take the shell, turn it over in her delicate palm, and with a twinkle in her eye, playfully pronounce, "It's a very nice shell, dear. Perhaps the second-best shell on the beach today." Ed would feign a dramatic sigh, and they'd continue their walk, hand in hand, the hunt for the perfect shell a sweet, simple strand in the tapestry of their days.

Still, evenings were the hardest. After a dinner of simple, savory sustenance, they'd settle in the living room. Photographs, precious portals to the past, populated every surface. There were the boys, gap-toothed and grinning in Little League uniforms. There were weddings, graduations, and the first fuzzy photos of their grandchildren. The faces smiled back, frozen in joyous frames, a beautiful but bittersweet reminder of the boisterous life they once led. Video calls with Boston and Boise were bright spots, but the ten-hour time difference to Hawaii made connecting with Bartholomew's bunch a complicated calculation. The loneliness would creep in then, a cool, quiet tide washing over the warmth of their love.

"It's silly, isn't it?" Sue-Ellen murmured one evening, tracing the face of her youngest grandson in a photo. "To have so much, to be so blessed, and still feel... a little bit bare."

Ed wrapped his arm around her. "It's not silly, Sue-Ellen. It's love. We're just so full of it, it has to go somewhere."

The week of Ed's seventy-first birthday dawned dazzling and bright. The air was alive with the scent of salt and sweet plumeria drifting on the breeze. Sue-Ellen had planned a simple, splendid day: a morning walk, a fine fish dinner at their favorite seaside spot, and a special strawberry shortcake, Ed's favorite.

They began their birthday beachcombing, the sun just beginning its spectacular ascent. The waves whispered sweet secrets to the shore. Ed, in his usual fashion, was scanning the sand for his elusive prize. He stooped, spotting a sand dollar of significant size. "Sue-Ellen, my sweet! Surely, this is it! The supreme sand dollar! The-"

He stopped mid-sentence. His eyes, and then Sue-Ellen's, were drawn to a peculiar point on the placid, purple-blue plane of the morning sea. A shape was moving toward them, steady and serene. It was too large to be a drifting log, too low to be a boat. As it drew nearer, its form became fantastically, unbelievably clear.

It was a colossal sea turtle, ancient and awesome, its powerful flippers paddling with a placid, purposeful rhythm. And on its broad, barnacle-studded back, it towed a tidy, trim little raft. On the raft, waving with wild, wonderful glee, were four small figures, their silhouettes sharp against the shimmering sea.

Ed's jaw dropped. Sue-Ellen's hands flew to her mouth, her gasp lost in the gentle roar of the surf. It was impossible. It was incredible. It was Bartholomew's bunch. It was Iokeline, Akelaika, Mikiala, and Elenola.

The grand turtle, with a final, graceful glide, guided the raft right to the shore, nudging it gently onto the wet sand. Four small pairs of feet hit the ground running.

"Grandpa! Grandma!"

The quiet of the Tampa coast was gloriously, gratifyingly shattered by the gleeful greetings of their grandchildren. Four small bodies slammed into them, a tidal wave of hugs and happiness. Ed found himself lifting little Elenola high in the air, her laughter a melody more magical than any birdsong. Sue-Ellen was enveloped by Akelaika and Mikiala, while Iokeline, the eldest, beamed, her smile as bright as the burgeoning day.

"Happy Birthday, Grandpa!" they chorused, a cacophony of cheer.

Bartholomew and his wife appeared as if from a dream, walking from a little way down the beach where they'd been waiting. The logistics, Bartholomew later explained with a laugh, involved a very early flight into Tampa International, a pre-arranged and perplexing pact with a particularly perceptive sea turtle (a long story involving a rescued fishing net and a shared love of sea grass), and a whole lot of hope.

The day was a whirlwind of wonder. Their quiet cottage was transformed into a castle of joyous chaos. The air filled with the sounds Ed and Sue-Ellen had missed so dearly: the pitter-patter of running feet, the shrieks of playful discovery, and the incessant, inquisitive "why?" that is the hallmark of a happy child. They built a fantastic fortress of furniture, read stories in silly voices until they were hoarse, and baked the strawberry shortcake with a chaotic committee of small, flour-dusted chefs.

For dinner, they didn't go out. They had a picnic on the living room floor—a fantastic feast of fish sticks and French fries, a meal more magnificent than any five-star fare. Ed, seated in the center of it all, felt a profound, perfect peace settle over him. The pang of loneliness was gone, replaced by an overwhelming, overflowing love. He caught Sue-Ellen's eye across the happy havoc, and she gave him a watery, wonderful smile that said everything.

As the afternoon sun began its slow, spectacular slide into the sea, painting the sky in strokes of orange, pink, and purple, it was time for the magical journey home. The great sea turtle had been waiting patiently in the shallows, munching on sea lettuce.

There were long hugs and promises of another visit soon. "Thank you for the best birthday ever, my little wonders," Ed said, his voice thick with emotion.

"We love you, Grandpa! We love you, Grandma!" they called, clambering back onto the raft.

With a final wave, the children were off. The ancient turtle began its powerful, placid paddle, pulling the raft away from the shore and into the heart of the fiery sunset. Ed and Sue-Ellen stood on the beach, arm in arm, watching until the little raft was just a speck against the vast, vibrant canvas of the sky. The house would be quiet again, but it was a different kind of quiet now. It was a peaceful quiet, filled with the echoes of laughter, the warmth of recent hugs, and the sweet, sticky memory of strawberry shortcake.

As the last sliver of the sun sank below the horizon, Ed's foot nudged something in the sand. He bent down and picked it up. It was a conch shell, flawlessly formed, its spiral a perfect poem of the sea. Its lip was lined with a shimmering, pearlescent pink that seemed to hold all the colors of the sunset they had just witnessed.

He held it out to his wife. "Sue-Ellen," he said softly.

She took it, her fingers tracing its exquisite form. She looked from the shell, to her husband's loving face, and back out to the empty, beautiful sea.

"Ed," she whispered, a tear of pure joy tracing a path down her cheek. "It's perfect."

29

I WISH

"What's that, Charlie?"

"It's a coin of some kind. But I've never seen anything quite like it."

"What does it say?"

"I dunno. It's in Latin or some other language. I have no idea what it says."

"You get that at work like the last fifteen coins and the rest of the stuff you brought home?"

Her voice clearly communicated her displeasure with his bringing home items that he found at work. Or elsewhere, for that matter.

"Yes, I found it in one of the fountains at the zoo. It looks cool, though. I like it."

Charlie and Melinda had a medium-sized home. Three bedrooms, two-and-a-half baths. The den had become Charlie's junk room by default, mostly because of the stuff he brought home from work. No matter what she tried, she wasn't able to persuade him to stop bringing the junk home. It's like he had an addiction. He couldn't not bring it home. He had to have it, had to share it with her, had to add it to "My Collection" as he called it.

"Aren't there some rules or laws that say you can't bring stuff home?" Melinda had asked more than once, hoping that there were.

"Yeah, there are. We have to keep stuff in the Lost & Found for thirty days. Every once in a while, someone will call and ask about what they left behind, but usually we never hear from them. After a month, the boss tells the crew we can take whatever we want, and most of the guys aren't interested."

Most of it seemed worthless, not even worth doing a yard sale or putting it on eBay or The Marketplace. One time, however, he came home with an expensive-looking camera. They looked it up online and ended up selling it for three thousand dollars. They used that money to pay off the car. He found a baseball card that seems to be worth a lot. A rookie card of one of his favorite players when he was a kid. Even though it is in mint condition, he's not interested in selling it. This just served to reinforce his addiction.

A week or so after coming home with the newest addition to his collection, they were in the car at a traffic light on the way to the mall. The light was red for a super long time, much longer than usual.

"What's the matter with it? I wish the light would turn green!" Charlie yelled.

Immediately, the light turned green. But they didn't think anything of it because they had been sitting at the intersection a long time.

The next day, he got a phone call from his neighbor, Bob, who was complaining about Charlie's lawn again. He cited HOA rules and was going to report him. The guy went on and on and on. And after hanging up the phone, Charlie said to Melinda, "I wish he'd just drop dead."

A week went by, and there was an email from the HOA saying there was going to be special election to fill the position that opened when Bob died suddenly of a heart attack.

Every time Charlie made a statement that included the words *I Wish,* things happened exactly like he said it. The airport added a runway, even though there was no budget for it. The governor was kidnapped and never heard from again. His baseball team had led the league in losses the past three seasons in a row, but went undefeated the next season. His boss was fired on the spot. At the age of thirty-eight, Charlie grew seven inches taller and Melinda's bust increased four inches.

People died, moved, disappeared, called on the phone, got jobs far away. The weather changed. Congress made new laws. The HOA disbanded. Their dog, who for years barked way too much, suddenly went mute. That's when Melinda began to realize something was going on. Things happened inexplicably. Almost miraculously.

"Charlie, I've noticed something."

"What's that, Gorgeous?"

"It seems every time you say *I Wish,* it happens."

"What are you talking about?"

She rattled off a list of twenty-five or thirty strange happenings in the past year that they had ignored as coincidences.

"About a month ago, I started making a list of weird things, and the list is pretty long. Then I thought back to when it all started, and it seems to go back to the day you brought that coin home from work."

"That's impossible," Charlie shot back.

"Maybe, but it's happening."

"Give me an example," he demanded.

"Okay. The day after you said you wished you had a college degree because you'd get a raise, there was a letter in the mail from the university awarding you a BS. Charlie, you dropped out after two semesters. But now you're a college graduate and you got the raise?"

"What else?"

"Well, since you asked. Do you know how tall you were when we got married? And how tall you are now?"

"That can be explained scientifically. Delayed Thyroid Activation caused by improved diet."

"So you grew seven inches in one day? No, Charlie. Something weird is happening. I want to look at that coin."

He went to the den and brought it out.

"What does it say?" she asked.

"Let's see if I can make out the words: *Possessoris huius nummi vota eius per quinquennium exaudientur.*"

"What does that mean, Charlie?"

"I wish I knew."

30

IF

One word. That's all it took to unravel a full year of negotiations. Until then, they had been working slowly but surely towards a mutual trust, both sides confident that the other was speaking and acting honestly and in good faith. But suddenly there was a crack in that confidence.

The day they were to sign and finalize the treaty, there was a joint news conference. The two ambassadors stood side by side, smiling. The first got up to speak, expressing gratitude to his counterpart for the work they had accomplished and a heartfelt relief that the war between the two nations would finally come to an end.

After the applause died down, the second ambassador went to the podium and began similarly. But three minutes and twelve seconds into his speech, he used a word that caused concern. As he spoke, he casually said, "if" we sign this treaty instead of "when" we sign this treaty, and that faux pas unraveled the trust and the confidence that had theoretically been established during the talks.

While the second ambassador continued talking, the first speaker pulled out his phone and texted his president, who gave the order to bomb the other nation's parliament where the members were in session and watching the news conference. They sent a missile to the residence of the president, who was home with his family and a few friends.

31

INCLEMENT WEATHER

As Girl Scout Troop 36 hiked through the Narrows of Zion National Park, a sudden flash flood roared in and caught them mid-stride, thunder cracking like gunfire while icy water surged past their ankles, forcing the girls to cling to one another and push through rising panic as they fought their way toward higher ground, the storm twisting their once-bright adventure into a desperate struggle for survival.

32

INHERITANCE

The newspapers called it a mansion. In truth, the family never saw it that way. Sure, it was a walled-in property with a security gate on the grounds and old ivy climbing up the corners of the house, but the home itself was only a six-bedroom, two-story house. There was a living room, a dining room, a music room, and a multipurpose room. Was that a "mansion?" I guess it depended on one's point of view. The family never saw it that way. It was just home.

It was a home that most of them had not visited in a while. The kids, a son and a daughter, had turned against their father years earlier, each for their own reasons. Children of privilege sometimes find reasons to lash out that children of lesser means would never even think about. And so, these two kids had left the nest, resentful of their successful father, each wanting a piece of what he had but not willing to put in the work to achieve what he had achieved.

The grandkids each had their own relationship with their grandfather. Their grandmother had passed away before any of them were born, so grandfather was all they knew from that side of the family. William, called Bill, was the oldest grandchild, the only child of the son. Then came Maxine and Martin, the children of the patriarch's daughter.

The patriarch was not dumb. He had been clever enough to build his empire from the ground up without any assistance. One could say he was actually quite astute with a keen eye for reading people. Because of this keen eye, he saw that he had erred in raising his two children. The love lost between them was a constant source of sorrow for the old man. Thus, he was always intentional to build strong connections with his grandchildren. Where he had failed as a father, he would succeed as a grandfather. This was not always easy. Children, being the product of their own homes, often take on the attitudes and inclinations of their parents. As such, the patriarch's grandchildren were unduly influenced by the negative emotions and memories of their parents towards the old man.

Only Martin genuinely loved the old man. Martin would spend every summer at the estate, hanging around his grandfather and listening intently to all of the old man's stories and wisdom. Bill and Maxine used to tease Martin, accusing him of sucking up to the old man in order to curry favor. But no one could deny that the affection between Martin and his grandfather was genuine. When the patriarch finally passed away, Martin was hit the hardest. The funeral was nearly unbearable, but they endured it as many families do, with a mixture of false and genuine remorse and mourning. Then came the day for the reading of the will.

The patriarch had used the same legal office for decades. When the attorney for Johnstone, Jonstone & Williams showed up to the house, the entire family was practically salivating to hear how the estate would be divvied up. The lawyer walked into the dining room and set his valise on the table. With a resounding CLICK, he unfastened the latch and pulled out some legal documents. His voice was deep with a slight nasal quality to it as he said:

"Your father and grandfather were quite clear in their instructions to my firm. Because of the animosity and disrespect directed towards him by his children over the past two decades, they receive no part of the estate in any way."

This caused an eruption from the son and daughter of the patriarch. "WHAT?!? This is not fair! He can NOT just write us out of his life and leave us with nothing!"

The lawyer continued, "As I stated, your father was quite clear and the matter is legally binding. You are receiving no part of his estate…except…"

"EXCEPT FOR WHAT?!?" yelled Bill and Maxine. The cousins were both wide-eyed and had veins bulging in their necks.

Martin shook his head. "Y'all need to chill, he was literally about to say it before you interrupted."

The lawyer, looking slightly perturbed, continued. "You are receiving no part of his estate except for one item of your choosing from within the house."

"THAT'S. IT?!?" Bill was furious. As the oldest of the cousins, he felt he had to take the lead to make things right. After all we've done, all of the 'Happy birthday, Grandpa!' phone calls we've made and ghastly visits we had to endure, we only get to pick ONE thing from inside this house?!?"

Martin smirked. "With all of the ungodly expensive things in this house, you should be grateful. You can take your one thing and make a small fortune off of it."

Bill looked furiously at his cousin. "Thanks, Pollyanna."

The lawyer continued, "After the three of you pick your items, everything else will be put into trust to be disseminated at a later time and place that does not concern anyone at this time and place. You have one hour to make your choices."

The house became a veritable tornado. Bill and Maxine tore through the house, looking for the single-most valuable item they could lay their hands on. Martin sighed and walked towards his grandfather's private study. Sixty minutes later, the three of them were standing back beside the attorney. Each had an item in their hands.

Bill held a small Renoir. He had estimated it was valued at $1–2 million at auction. Maxine had made it to the jewelry collection in the house. She found an art deco emerald necklace she was sure she could unload for six figures.

Martin stood there holding a small, hand carved box. His cousins looked at him disdainfully. He looked at them, sadness filling his face.

"You don't recognize this box? Grandpa bought it for Grandma for one of their anniversaries. He picked it up when he was a traveling salesman. He didn't have much, and he found this at a flea market. She kept it for their whole marriage. Even after she died, he said he would never part with it. It reminded him of a simpler time when all they had was each other."

And that was that.

The cousins parted ways, looking forward to getting back to real life and the problems and issues that came with it. Bill was able to offload the Renoir for a pretty penny. It wasn't the inheritance he had hoped for, but at least he wasn't a schmuck like his cousin. Maxine, likewise, was able to sell the necklace to a collector. Martin, though, was a different story.

Martin had no intention of selling the box. He loved it because of what it represented of his grandparents and their connection. He had grown up seeing it in his grandfather's study every time he visited. His grandfather would tell him stories about life on the road as a traveling salesman and coming home to his wife and kids, exhausted from the trips but thrilled to be back with family.

As Martin looked at the box one evening, he slid his hand along the underside where the edges didn't seem to match up. Suddenly, a small compartment popped open. A secret compartment no more than a half inch wide. Martin, filled with curiosity, pulled the drawer open. Inside was a slip of paper, and on that slip of paper someone wrote 21 characters, a mix of letters and numbers. A secret Swiss bank account number had been stored inside the anniversary box.

Martin had no idea how long the paper had been there. He needed to investigate, so his first call was to his grandfather's attorney.

"Congratulations, Martin!" The attorney sounded positively ecstatic. Everything your grandfather owned was put into a trust, and all of the documents controlling that trust are part of that Swiss bank account. Your grandfather wanted whoever found value in the box to know that it represented all he truly found valuable in the world. Now your grandfather's estate passes to you."

33

IGNITING A FIRE

How on earth am I going to turn this team around?

Jesse had just arrived to Tulsa, Oklahoma after a decade of success as a Texas high school football coach. His team in Midlands, Texas had drawn 15,000 fans every Friday night and now here he was in Tulsa, in a stadium built for 30,000 that seemed mostly empty every Saturday. Maybe they had 8,000. If they hit 10K he would be surprised.

So now the task of rebuilding…not even that, just building a team that could bring a spark to the community. Jesse didn't even care about how many wins he would get. He just wanted to bring some excitement. This town had faced declining population, declining economy, declining life for far too long. Jesse took it as his personal mission to inject life back into the community through his football team.

Should he focus on recruiting new players? Reach back out to his connections in Texas to get quality players? But how do you sell Tulsa OK, to top recruits who have places like UT Austin, Ohio State, or even Texas Tech on their radar?

On his first day out on the practice field he felt like a combination of the Water Boy, Ted Lasso, and The Longest Yard. Trying to figure out how to motivate and inspire a bunch of kids who were struggling to put together a coherent offense and defense.

One thing he knew, is that he would never give up. He had hope. He knew that with the right talent, the right training, the right team spirit, they could ignite a fire in Tulsa and bring excitement back to the community.

Ok he told himself. Down to business.

34

IN-LAWS

Jake needed this job, but he had to have his own tools. He knew how to do all kinds of carpentry, but having the right equipment was crucial, and right now he didn't have the money to buy anything and the job was supposed to start next Monday and he really needed a circular saw. But having been without a job most of the past year, credit cards were maxed out, checks were bouncing beyond the roofline, and bill collectors were on a first-name basis.

He and Lizzy had only been married a few years. What started with happiness and hope had soon devolved into sadness because of their situation. They didn't have much hope right now, and certainly couldn't afford to celebrate Jake's birthday next Saturday. Thursday night, Lizzy's mother called and invited them over for lunch the next day.

"Right now's not a good time, Mom. We're going through a rough spot and I'm not sure Jake is up for it."

"Well, honey, you need to eat, so talk about it and let me

know, okay?"

"Okay, Mom."

Lizzy ended the call and found Jake in the garage.

"My mom called. They invited us over for lunch tomorrow. Wanna go?"

"No."

"Wanna talk?"

"No."

"We have to eat and we don't have any money and you know they love us."

"But I feel so embarrassed. I hate being with anybody."

"Even family?"

"Yes. Especially family. But hey. You're right. We gotta eat. And they do love you, even though you married a loser."

"Jake, is that how you feel?"

"Yes."

"Well, it's not how I see you."

When they showed up at her parents' home, lunch was on the table, and a nicely-wrapped present sat on the floor in the corner. After they ate, Lizzy's mom brought out a cake. She lit the candles and they all sang Happy Birthday. Then she scooped the ice cream while Lizzy's dad brought the gift to the table. Lizzy had a tear in her eye when Jake opened it and discovered a brand-new skill saw.

35

IT'S IN MY BLOOD

Jean-Louis was born in Mézel, France, but grew up in Vineland, New Jersey. His parents had moved the family to America in 1884 when he was three, after an unexpected parasite killed all of their vines. His father's family had been the leading vintners in the region for almost three centuries, but after losing the vines, he became bitter, sold the land, and wanted nothing to do with wine or winemaking. Jean-Louis's father was now a production manager at Welch's, overseeing the grape fields for their juice, but for the rest of his life, he was adamant about avoiding wine and all alcohol, just like Mr. Welch.

Jean-Louis, on the other hand, was sick of grape juice, and resented not being able to enjoy some wine once in a while. More than once, during an argument with his father, he shouted, "When I grow up, I'm going to grow my own grapes and make my own wine." Ironically, his parents had never told him of their family's history of winemaking in the hills around Mézel.

As fate would have it, without telling his parents, during his senior year of high school, Jean-Louis applied to attend Cal Poly San Luis Obispo, a new university on the West Coast, and was accepted into their Viticulture and Winemaking program.

"Perfect," he told a friend. "I can escape from my parents and pursue what I really want to do with my life. This is my calling, my destiny, it's in my blood."

36

J WILLIAM RICHARDSON III ESQ

J. William Richardson III, Esq., left his home in rural Louisiana at the age of fourteen, determined never to look back. Nothing his family did quite qualified as abuse, but if the constant negativity, partial neglect, and persistent sense of unwelcome—how they tore him down whenever he achieved even the smallest success—helped him make up his mind. If he didn't get out from under them, they would keep him down forever.

"Camo," as his childhood friends used to call him, had a lifelong tendency to keep his head down, in large part due to the metaphorical bucket of crabs he used to live in. His fondness for avoiding the lime light did not stop him from graduating with honors, first from Northeast High School, then Louisiana State University, and finally LSU-Baton Rouge School of Law. His concentration in corporate tax law suited his sharp mind for numbers and his obsessive-compulsive need to cross Ts, dot Is, and balance the books.

It might not come as much of a shock, despite the awful pun, that Camo Richardson (camouflage riches) accumulated stealth wealth—something in the ballpark of $27 million across sundry investment vehicles. From what Horatio Alger might call "unrespectable circumstances", the respectful young man made good on the American Dream, and a mere few years after graduating law school, through hard work and smart investing, was far from his upbringing, but could never get past his insecurities and need to escape it.

With his affluence, and while maintaining a low profile, Camo travelled the world, volunteering with various Non-Governmental Organizations and self-funding a few missions and outreach trips. That's where his rags to riches story stops cold. On the return flight from a trip to provide aid in the Central African Republic, his plane was lost at sea somewhere off the western coast of Africa.

Missing and presumed dead, a new cast of characters enter the scene.

Dr. Denis Mukwege Foundation joined by the **World Food Programme**: Charitable Non-Governmental Organizations (NGO) operating in the Central African Republic (CAR).

Maddison: The high school girlfriend that claims Camo fathered her child before he left for college.

Jed Michaels: The flat-fee attorney hired by Camo's siblings.

Isabella: The fiancé.

Each party showed up with assorted claims, all questionable, and all with the support of the law . . . but which law would hold out.

The NGOs claim that Camo created a will during his month-long aid visit prior to his demise, leaving all of his estate to support the causes after death that he most vigorously supported during life.

The state of Louisiana recognizes "Forced Heirship," where dependents under the age of 24 (or disabled) automatically inherit a portion of the estate regardless of any will or previously expressed interests of the deceased. Maddison claims that Camo is the biological father of her 7.5-year-old twins and she is entitled to half of the estate – 25% for each child (up to two) in accordance with state law.

Jed Michaels holds out that there is no will, the dearly departed had no children (legitimate or otherwise), and that the current-est girlfriend is trumping up their relationship in a ploy to secure the estate of the decedent.

Isabella, by far the most likable of the characters, lived in Baton Rouge. She was a special needs teacher in one of the local elementaries, but she and Camo went to the same church, and grew a fond respect for each other on a missions trip to Cameroon two summers ago. They officially began dating last year and Camo proposed to her last Christmas. They spent the summer in Colorado, renting a condo in the Springs near where Isabella's family lives. According to Isabella, they held themselves out as married and Camo intended to move his practice to Colorado. While Louisiana does not recognize common law marriage as occurring in-state, it does recognize common law marriages from other states. Colorado has the least restrictive relevant laws, and holding themselves out as married, cohabitating, let alone their pious background and unlikeliness to live together outside of marriage are all more than enough for Colorado to recognize the marriage.

Trial was set, the parties' lawyers notified, and everything in place for what promised to be the most exciting family case of the year. Things had already gotten nasty in the lead-up to getting a slot on the docket.

That's when the message came in:

International freight ship THE MERIDIEN TRADER reports finding a man stranded on a desert isle. Man claims to be J. William Richardson III., of Louisiana.

Isabella seemed to be the only one excited about the headlines.

37

JUST ONE MORE

The last few days, the weather had been terrible. Snow blowing sideways. Howling winds. Sub-zero temperatures. Zero visibility. The worst blizzard in over a decade.

But today…

Today was perfect. Temps in the 40's. Crisp but not freezing. Bright sunshine. Clear Skies. And the powder! The powder could not have been better. Not only was it now clear, but the unpredictable weather had kept most of the tourists away from the mountain!

Not only were there hardly any skiers, but this resort had been upgraded to the latest technology and most of the lifts were automated. Cameras and computers watched the loading areas. Customers moved through the entrance gates with radio-scanned ID cards and cameras would automatically slow or even stop the lifts if there were delays or people struggling to get on the chairs. It was remarkable and made for an almost surreal experience of snowboarding bliss!

Jeremy and Rick had the entire ski resort to themselves. They spent all day carving down the slopes, only to get to the bottom and immediately get on the lifts back to the top. Plenty of fresh snow, unmolested by the rich out-of-towners who usually clogged the runs like cholesterol in a fat man's veins. Just as unwanted, just as dangerous. The two local snowboarders reveled in the freedom of wide open carving in the sun.

As the day wore on they knew that the lifts would be shutting down soon. With very few patrons, and particularly this early in the year, the resort would be shutting down at dark. Around 5PM Jeremy motioned to Rick from across the mountain. Rick continued down the hill and hit a berm, executing a 360 degree twist with a forward flip. After sticking the landing he wished there were more people on the mountain at least to watch him and see how great he was.

Jeremy came shooting down the basin and whooshed to a stop right in front of Rick.

"Hey man, it's starting to get dark. We'd better get going before they shut things down."

"Yeah but we've got time for one more run! Let's get back on the lift quick before it's too late!"

The friends were so caught up in enjoying themselves they didn't pay attention to the warnings that the lifts were about to be shut down. Breezing through the empty lanes to the chair entrance, they only thought of how much fun the day had been.

The hum of the cable moving gracefully over the pillars was barely noticeable. And then…a mellow grinding far away.... The chairs came to a stop... Jeremy and Rick looked at each other, then at the ground 40 feet below.

Rick pulled out his phone to try to call for help. Zero bars. No reception.

"Oh shit. We're fucked." Were the words that went through their minds that neither of them were willing to say out loud.

The best friends tried to remain calm as they thought through their options.

The sun continued to sink over the peaks of the mountains. Darkness set in. The "warm" 40 degree temperature quickly dropping by the minute as the energy of the daylight gave way to the vacuum of darkness.

"We've gotta go for help."

"We are 40 feet in the air!"

"The snow will break our fall if we jump!"

"Whaaaaat??? That's insane!"

"Ok ok ok. Let's think! The lodge has to be keeping track of customers somehow. They've gotta figure out that we never came back for final check in off the mountain."

"Dude, those people don't make enough money to pay attention. We are stuck out here."

As they argued, the last bit of daylight flickered out and the world became darkness. No moon. No lights. Just cold, dark, night.

"What's that? Did I hear a howl? Are there freakin wolves out there?"

"Dude you are paranoid!"

"Oh man what are we gonna do?"

"Well I'm not gonna sit here and freeze to death"

And with that, Rick heaved himself off the chair lift, and dropped down into the darkness.

38

LIFE SENTENCE

When the testimonies, presentations of evidence, cross-examinations, and closing arguments were over, the jury sequestered themselves to deliberate, and the judge returned to his chambers to ruminate because the facts of the case were incredibly reminiscent of what his family had experienced and he was traumatized all over again, making it difficult to be objective, and he had a tough choice to make: recuse himself or finish the trial, which he could do, of course, but thinking about it made him wonder if that would be best for the people involved in this case, including himself, and by extension, his wife and kids, which brought a thousand more concerns and a deep angst which he wasn't quite sure how to handle, even after all these years on the bench, leading him to question whether he had ever been the right man for the job, the right man for his wife and family, the right man to enjoy all that life had given him, so he stopped and prayed for forgiveness before removing the pistol from his desk.

39

LIKE FATHER, LIKE SON

I don't remember growing old. I mean, I don't FEEL old, at least not in my head. My body, though, now that's a different story. My body tells me every day that I'm not the young guy my brain thinks it is. The long, hot shower helps the body and the brain. It soothes my aching, tired body and gives me time to pause and prep for the day. Every day now I hear Danny Glover's voice from Lethal Weapon in my head, "I'm too old for this ____." It's on repeat.

I step out of the shower, the small bathroom now filled with steam. My wife calls out from the other room, "Are you finally going to shave today? You haven't shaved all weekend!" The calm stillness that I had been living in while letting the piping hot water cover me is now shattered, a fragile balloon popped by the realities of life. "YES! I told you I was going to shave and I will."

I take the hand towel we keep by the bathroom sink and wipe off the steamy mirror and I'm startled to see my father looking back at me. I'm not old enough to look like Dad. My wife pops her head into the bathroom. "What are you staring at?"

Still looking in the mirror, I ask her, "When did we get old?" She laughs good-naturedly at me. "We passed middle-age years ago. We're on the backside of life now." I glance over at her. "Are you trying to hurt my feelings?" She sticks her tongue out at me and disappears back into the bedroom.

I turn and look at my dad again. I remember one time when I was a kid. Dad told me that he didn't like his nose. The nose he got from his dad. Now that nose is on the face in my mirror. I don't mind the nose, it's just funny to think about. I see less of me every day. Standing with one hand on the sink exactly like Dad used to do, I sigh, turn on the water, and get out my razor.

Here's to us, old man.

40

A LITTLE KINDNESS AND COMPASSION

A dozen scarlet roses greeted her as Bridget walked in the door. The bouquet was an opulent curation of long-stemmed, high-perfection roses in a hand-tied arrangement with baby's breath and other greens. Each rose carefully selected and symmetrical and the colors so vibrant, the contrast to her subtle pastel décor was stark. It was easily $600-worth of flowers sitting on her Ikea table in her small but comfortable apartment.

The card in the flowers read: "I will never forget the day we met, nor how I've fallen more and more in love with you every day since. You enthrall me. The fragrance of your perfume lingers in my mind, and the way you walk leaves me distracted thinking about you. Thank you for being in my life. ~Terry"

The knock on the door startled her as she was reading the note. Sliding the dime-size cover off the peep hole, Bridget placed one hand lightly on the door and leaned into to identify the visitor. It was a middle-aged, stocky man, with a neatly trimmed beard and she could smell the muddled mix of Pine-sol, tobacco, and WD-40 just looking at him. Tony was the apartment Super. A kindly and responsive man that was quick to make repairs and kept the whole place running like clockwork—even if he was always smoking on the roof when not in the service areas of the building.

Bridget opened the door and offered a polite but colder-than-normal greeting. Tony hesitated for a moment, perhaps taken aback by the lack of warm small talk like he usually shared with most of the residents. Shrugging it off, he continued. Glancing over Bridget's shoulder and into the apartment at the extravagant flower display on the table, he made eye contact with Bridget.

"Sorry to bother. Just wanted to make sure you got the flowers. They were delivered to the building, but I didn't want to just leave them down by the mailboxes in the common area. I went ahead to put them in the room for you. They came in the vase and look trimmed. The water's a bit cloudy, so I assume it already has the plant food stuff in it that often comes with flowers. Anyway, what's the special occasion? Not to be nosey, but I don't recall seeing anyone around, and that looks like a nice anniversary bouquet."

Bridget looked back over her shoulder at the flowers, but didn't say anything.

"I'm Sorry. I suppose it's none of my business. You have a great day, miss. Let me know if you need anything." Tony left, cheerfully greeting the residents four doors down that were coming out as he passed them in the hall.

Bridget walked over to the window and looked out the blinds. A moment later she closed them and walked back over to the table with the flowers. Ever since showing a bit of kindness and compassion to help that smarmy IT guy pick up the tools and miscellany that he dropped when the office bully tripped him, Terry wouldn't leave her alone. He'd done something to remote into her computer and arrange all her desktop icons into a heart. The calendar on her office wall seemed askew and was turned to the wrong month. And he'd friend-requested her on Facebook. He was quickly demonstrating all four signs of a stalker: fixated, obsessive, unwanted, and repeated.

And now the flowers . . . He knew her address.

41

LOVE GURU

"Maaaaan, did you see the way Samantha was looking at me in class?!?"

At 16 years old, all Jason cared about was girls. He was driving his dad's old Chevy S-10 pickup truck with his best friend, Mark, sitting right beside him.

"Yeah, I saw her, dude. She looked…what's the word? Disgusted." Mark couldn't believe they were having this conversation again. Sure, he was interested in finding a girlfriend, but he didn't obsess like Jason did. It was like Jason did literally nothing else than think about girls.

"No way, bro. She was DEFINITELY interested." Samantha may not have been the cutest girl in their class, but she was certainly in the running. "I know that look. She was into me!"

"I think you need help distinguishing interest and ick. That was one hundred percent the ick." Mark didn't think his friend would actually listen to him, but as the best friend it was his job – no, it was his duty – to speak the truth to Jason. He went on. "Besides, how do you even know what love looks like? You've never had a girlfriend for more than a week!"

Jason looked slightly hurt. "I know what love looks like."

"Oh, REALLY?! Do tell, oh love guru. How do you know what love looks like?" Mark rolled his eyes so hard he gave himself a small headache. The bumpy dirt road and Jason's wild driving didn't help his poor head.

Jason smiled slyly. "I know what love looks like because I listen to the radio!" Without skipping a beat he crooned in his best Elton John voice, "*Can you feel the love tonight*?"

Mark pressed his lips together and squinted at his friend. Jason didn't stop. Next was Whitney Houston. "AND IIIIIIIII-EE-IIIIIII-EE-III WILL ALWAYS LOVE YOU!"

"You're an idiot." Mark couldn't hide the grin breaking out on his face.

Jason kicked it up a notch and belted as loud as he could, "SHOT THROUGH THE HEART AND YOU'RE TO BLAME DARLIN' YOU GIVE LOVE A BAD NAME!"

Mark burst out laughing. "You know song lyrics, I'll give you that. I'll never believe you ACTUALLY know what love looks like."

42

LOVERS ISLAND

The invitations were sent two months ago. The venue confirmed weeks before that. The caterer delivered the food early. The preacher was there with the marriage license. The photographer was at the scene, the DJ already in full swing. Jeremy and Angela were ready to get married, but something was wrong.

No guests or relatives? Not even their parents?

Jeremy walked out to the vacant parking lot. The normally busy boulevard was totally empty, not a single car going either direction. Then in the distance he noticed multiple plumes of smoke rising over the mainland, and another a little closer. He pulled out his phone, opened the news app, and saw the headline.

Bridge to Lovers Island Bombed
in Early Stages of War

43

LUCY

Lucy was 12 years old when she finally learned what real love looks like. Born to teenage parents, Alexis and Joshua, who often reminded her she was an accident, Lucy grew up knowing she wasn't wanted. Like over half the babies born in New Mexico, her parents weren't married, but for a little while, it seemed like something was keeping them together.

When she was 8, she realized her dad was selling drugs. Her mom gripped her shoulders, fear sharp in her voice, "Don't ever tell anyone. If you do, they'll come take Joshua away, and they'll hate and despise us. Promise me you'll never tell a soul!"

Her breath hitched, tears blurring everything as she choked out, "I won't. I won't. I promise!"

When she was 10, Joshua got picked up near her school for possession with intent to distribute and sent to prison for three years. After shouting things she couldn't take back and collapsing into a shaking heap on the floor, Alexis rose without a word, went into her room, and slammed the door. That evening, Lucy poured herself a bowl of cereal, the clink of the spoon echoing in the quiet house. She brushed her teeth and changed her clothes with the same somber silence before crawling into her bed, feeling quite alone. In the morning, Alexis was gone.

She went to school and told her teacher about it, who told the principal, who called child services. Whispers rippled through the classroom. Lucy's stomach dropped, and her already fragile ego was shattered when her situation was made public in front of her class and child services took her into custody. "Taken into custody" may not be the preferred phrase for people to use, but that's what it felt like to her.

Forms, questions, waiting rooms—everything felt endless through a bureaucratic maze she'd never imagined. It didn't seem like the same level of detail applied to would-be foster parents. What was likely only a couple of days in reality felt like an eternity before she was placed into short-term foster care. Seven other kids lived there, with an unspoken hierarchy she learned quickly, all away from the unobservant eyes of Rick and Debby.

The next two years saw her moved to three different homes with feeble excuses or justification if any. Nevertheless, here she was, a 12-year-old mistake that nobody wanted, nobody cared about, and no real chance of happiness.

That's when she arrived at Daniel and Karen's home. One child of their own that was about grown and out of the house, and two infant foster kids—actual brother and sister. The older kid was essentially non-existent in her life, and while Dan was out working, Karen largely had her hands full with the little 'uns.

Karen seemed to know what was going on in the house and always had a watchful eye, even though she was very hands off. A few days into her stay, Lucy walked from the pantry with a box of cereal. She stood in the kitchen, unsure where anything was, until Karen quietly pointed out the silverware while setting a bowl on the counter. After the first month, Lucy relaxed a little, but didn't want to get too comfortable. It was only a matter of time before she'd be forced to move again.

Once Lucy seemed to let down her guard, Karen started trying to be a lot more involved. No yelling, no belittling, and apparently genuine interest in Lucy. It was weird. Lucy didn't quite know what to do with it. But then again, she didn't know much about life. Everything was uncertain, everything was unfair.

She didn't try to be a problem, but trouble seemed to follow her, and she regularly found herself sent to the office or threatened with detention. Nor did she try to pick fights with Dan and Karen. It just sort of happened. She knew it was only a matter of time until they pushed her out and she would have to go to another home.

But Dan and Karen gently and firmly applied more rules and guidelines, more restrictions, and got more involved in her life. What was with them?

Then the night came that Dan and Karen asked her to come have a seat in the living room. "This is it. This is where they tell me I can't live here anymore and that they don't want me." Lucy was sure of it.

[Karen] "Lucy. We both want to talk with you. We know life hasn't been fair. It hasn't been easy. And you've had to deal with things that no kid should ever have to deal with. It's hard. It'd be hard for anyone."

[Lucy] "Yeah, yeah. Just skip to the part where you kick

me out and send me off to some other home."

[Dan] "What? No, no . . . nothing like that. We want to let you know that no matter how hard you push us away, we're not giving up on you. We're here for you, and we wish you would share with us what's going on. What's it like in your new school? Who are your friends?"

Lucy rolled her eyes, failing to suppress her doubt of Dan's sincerity, all the while wanting it to be true. The tense "family meeting" itself would be enough to drive most young girls to tear up, and Lucy was no different in that regard. The dissonance between her expectations and what Dan and Karen were saying added confusion that also showed through her moist eyes. "You say that now." She swallowed hard—her throat felt thick.

[Karen] "We'll say it tomorrow, too." After a brief pause, Karen continued, "It seemed like you were finally starting to relax a little, and then you started acting out."

[Lucy] "Maybe I don't want to stay here. After all, you've been getting meaner and meaner and not letting me do much of anything anymore."

[Dan] "Lucy. Real love sets boundaries. Real love is unconditional. It's because we care about you that Karen and I have started cracking down and setting stricter rules.

Lucy scoffed and let loose another eye roll, this time avoiding eye contact afterward while trying to process what was actually being said.

[Dan] "We're trying to be fair with the consequences and match them to your behaviors and tendencies. We want you to thrive, but people only grow and develop the right way when there is structure and guidance. That's why we've added all the additional systems.

[Lucy] "You don't love me. Nobody could love me. I was an accident . . . a mistake! How could anyone ever love a bastard like me?"

[Karen] "Did you know that one of the most famous stories in the world starts with an unplanned pregnancy and a couple that wasn't yet married?"

[Lucy] *Sniffling* "Really?"

[Dan] "It sure does. Has anyone ever told you the story about Mary and Joseph, and their baby named Jesus?"

[Lucy] "You mean, like that church stuff? I've heard something about it, but it's just that sissy stuff to make people scared to do bad things."

[Karen] "Some might talk poorly about it, and as for it being a gentle and forgiving religion, you're right. But it's not about doing good things because you fear hell; it's about loving God so much you want to do good things. The Bible even talks about strength and power and all the ways that God helps us. But it all starts with his love for us. The story of Jesus' time on Earth isn't all sunshine and roses, and despite Him trying to teach everyone to love each other and take care of each other, many people hated Him. They didn't want to let go of their hate and treat others well.

[Dan] "But he loved all of them—even those that hated Him or tried to hurt Him. God loves US unconditionally, and sets rules for us to follow because of that love. He sets the perfect example of what real love looks like. Can we tell you the story?"

[Lucy] "I'm not really sure. I mean . . . I don't know."

Karen didn't move closer, but she angled her body slightly toward Lucy, leaving space—an invitation, not a demand. Lucy noticed, not even pretending she didn't.

After a long moment, Lucy scooted an inch closer on the couch. Not touching—just... nearer. Testing. Waiting to see if Karen would flinch or shift away.

Karen didn't.

[Lucy][Barely above a whisper] "I don't . . . I don't know how to do this."

[Karen] "You don't have to know. I'm here."

Lucy nodded once, tiny and stiff. She let her shoulder tilt a little toward Karen—not leaning, not cuddling, just letting gravity pull her a fraction closer. Karen didn't move, didn't comment, didn't make it weird.

Lucy exhaled shakily. "Can I… just sit here? Like this?"

Karen smiled softly. "Of course."

Lucy didn't look up, but she let herself stay there—close enough to feel the warmth of someone who wasn't leaving.

Not trust. Not yet. But a beginning.

44

MIDDLEMIST'S RED

There it was again.

Flashing bright against the black velvet lining of the wall safe.

A small but distinct red flower.

Why?

Archie Lorrenz was a detective in the City of London. Having grown up on the east side of London in Dagenham, Archie had performed exceptionally well in school and was also a star athlete on the track. It wasn't that he was exceptionally fast, but that he picked the middle distances to compete and he had an uncanny ability to overpower his lungs and muscles with his mind and run full speed far beyond when most men would start listening to their bodies and give up. His unwavering determination is what helped propel him past his blue collar upbringing and rise to detective for the City of London, solving crimes for the elites.

This was the third burglary in the last two months where the thief had left a calling card of sorts. And the calling card presented a mystery almost as complex as how the break ins were pulled off without a trace. The flower left at the scene, was the most rare flower in the world. The Middlemist's Red Camellia.

The Middlemist's Red originated in China and was brought to Europe in the early 1800's but no longer exists in Asia. It is so rare that only two known flowers exist in the world. One is in New Zealand on the grounds of the historic house where the treaty between the British and the original natives of New Zealand was signed. The other flower… right here in London at the Chiswick House and Gardens.

This was a challenge to the police flaunting how unique the thief believed himself to be. Not only could he not be caught through ordinary investigative means, he left a clue so rare and specific it had to be traceable… and yet... still nothing.

Archie was troubled but determined. No fingerprints. No signs of forced entry. Nothing caught on cameras. And the owners of the residences were rich elites who were out of town and showed no signs of fraud or criminal intent. The entire crime scenes were clean. Except for this flower.

Archie visited the Chiswick House to talk to the head curator and botanist Angela Baxter.

"No, you can't examine the Middlemist's Red. It's too rare."

It took a full month of working through official channels to even be allowed to inspect the plant at Chiswick.

When Archie arrived at the museum grounds again, he was greeted by a begrudging Ms. Baxter.

"Get into these coveralls. Put on this mask. And for heaven's sake, make sure you don't actually touch the flower!"

After twenty minutes of close scrutiny Archie had nothing. He sighed deeply.

"Any records of when the flower first came to London?"

The reluctant curator took him to a dusty office and thumped a large ancient book on the desk. It took some time carefully digging through the book, but eventually he found it. The flower had come to London from China in 1804. But the records showed purchase of a cutting from the flower by one Thomas Baring. It was removed to be regrown and given to Napoleon as a thank you for using Baring Brothers & Co as the facilitating financial institution for the Louisiana Purchase. The flower was to be presented at Napoleons coronation in 1805 but it never made it out of London. Some notes scribbled on the old document revealed that the cutting had disappeared before it could be given to Baring. As it was meant to be a gift to the enemy of England, Baring never pursued the matter with authorities.

Inspector Lorrenz was back to square one. How could this flower cutting have survived from 1804 all the way to today without ever being discovered? Who could have access to it? And why use it to taunt the police at the scene of these crimes?

With the trail to the antique flower dried up, all he could do was wait for the next break in and hope the thief made a mistake.

45

MOM'S FLUTE

Phyllis didn't care about the money. It was nice, but that's not what mattered. She missed her mom. She missed hearing Mom talk. She missed Mom's music. So when she and her brothers met to read the will and divvy up the stuff, all she really wanted was Mom's flute.

She remembered lying in bed as a seven-year-old and falling asleep to the sound of arpeggios, melodies, and children's songs. Mom was a flutist in the local symphony and would often play what she called fluff pieces after the kids went to bed.

It was pretty cut and dried that everyone would get the same amount of money. But the simple will didn't discuss furnishings, jewelry, clothing, or art. The house was to be sold and the proceeds split evenly. But what about the stuff?

Much of the discussion focused on the art because some of it was valuable—original oils, pottery, and bronzes. Her brother, John, had become an art dealer and knew the approximate value of each piece. Peter was a musician, but a cellist, so he didn't particularly care who got the flute. Fred was a real estate attorney and would handle the property sale. Phyllis was a history professor at the local state university. Her doctoral studies had focused on the transition of the Austrian Empire to the Austro-Hungarian Empire. But mostly, she missed her mom.

The siblings took turns declaring what they wanted, and the session was quite amicable. They all discussed what each item might be worth, but the value of the stuff was of pretty low importance. Each of them had other reasons for what they wanted: when and where Mom had acquired it, whether they liked it, and what it reminded them about Mom. And they all agreed that what they walked away with was final, there'd be no arguing later or fighting about who got what and what turned out to be worth more. Fred even provided the agreement for them all to sign . . . and they did.

A few days later, Phyllis's husband and kids were away for a few hours, so she took out her mom's flute. She wasn't a musician, but she had watched Mom so many times that she pretty much knew what to do, so she picked it up and blew into it. It seemed something was obstructing the airflow, so she looked into the end of the flute and found a rolled-up piece of paper.

Using a pair of tweezers, she pulled it out, trying not to rip whatever it was. Slowly, carefully, gently tugging at what seemed to be an old piece of paper. Finally, the whole scroll was out, a letter from her mother, accompanied by a small key.

My Dear Phyllis: I know how you enjoyed hearing me play when you were a little girl, so I hope you are the one reading this note. I love you so much and want you to have the instrument I played. In much the same way my music touched your heart, you are the music that touched mine. The key is to a safe deposit box at my bank. I wanted the contents to be yours because I think it will mean something to you. Whether you keep it, sell it, or give it away is entirely up to you. All my love, Mother.

On Monday, Phyllis's first class wasn't until early afternoon, so she took the key and went to the bank. There in the box was an original piece of music for flute: handwritten, signed, and dated by Ludwig Van Beethoven, 1815.

There was also a note: "Receive this as a token of gratitude for your participation in and promotion of the Vienna Beethoven Society. The music is authentic. It has been certified by the Viennese Historical Society." The seal of the society was intact.

Phyllis cried and smiled and gasped all at the same time, and the bank manager standing at the door hurried over to see if she was all right.

46

THE MOST SIGNIFICANT YEAR

"I lost count of how many times I've fallen off the wagon," Betty lamented to herself. "There's something comforting about a box of wine after a long, trying day… and something troubling about using an entire box to cope with just about anything—well, anything except a family reunion or game night. But I digress. I do love boxed wine."

The problem wasn't the drinking itself, nor even knowing when to stop. She never went to work drunk or hungover, but most nights had blurred together for nearly three years, and she needed it to end. Betty and James were two years married when they conceived, two and a half when she miscarried, and three when he filed for divorce.

"It feels like a lifetime ago—and also like yesterday. I remember the newlywed butterflies, the joy of saying 'We're pregnant,' 'We're having a baby,' all the 'we's.' And I remember the blame that followed—the 'You lost the baby,' all the 'you's.' So many memories packed into such a short time."

Their first anniversary was a delight; they'd never really left the newlywed phase. Their second anniversary was joyful and hopeful. Even without a positive test, they were trying. Shortly after the second anniversary, Betty peed on a stick, and both their hearts lit up with glee.

Now, two and a half years divorced, Betty had a different kind of milestone to celebrate. Losing the baby was the worst. James's betrayal was unexpected and cruel, though he'd never truly been the dependable-for-life kind of man. Perhaps it was better she learned the truth early—but the timing was unbearably unfair. It took a year and a half to hit rock bottom. Only then could she face her life and begin clawing her way back.

For the longest while she blamed herself. Lord knows that James blamed her. But after losing control for so long, it felt like an act of God that kept her from going over the edge and finally brought her back to her senses. "Thank you, God, for helping me to see things clearly."

She had been sober for 363 days. Tomorrow would be huge!

She told her girlfriends only two weeks before the event; she'd tried to get sober three times before and always fallen off the wagon. This time was different, and the only difference was God.

She'd stumbled into a midweek service at the church down the road. They were hosting small groups and had a ladies' group that was meeting that night. Had it been any other night, or any other church, or perhaps the Mormon ward across the street, who knows where her life would be right now had it not been for that moment.

Tomorrow would mark 364 days—one day shy of a full year since she chose to stop drowning the grief of losing her baby, her marriage, and nearly herself. The miscarriage had hollowed her out, and James's blame had carved the hollow even deeper. For a long time, she believed she deserved the emptiness. For a long time, she believed she had caused it.

But tomorrow, she would stand among women who had held her story without flinching. Women who didn't blame her. Women who didn't leave. Women who reminded her that healing rarely happens alone.

Her sobriety wasn't just a milestone; it was a resurrection of the self she thought had died the day the pregnancy test turned negative and the marriage papers turned final. And maybe that was the miracle—God meeting her in the lowest place and walking her back into the light, one trembling step at a time.

She didn't know what the next year would hold—joy, sorrow, something in between—but she knew she would meet it sober, awake, and wholly herself. She knew she would carry the memory of her baby with tenderness instead of shame. She knew she could think of James without collapsing.

Maybe that was enough.

And for anyone listening, anyone aching, anyone whispering into the dark:

You are not alone. Someone will hear you. Someone will stay. Someone will help you rise again.

47

NIGHT JOB

It wasn't that he LIKED working nights. No, scratch that. He actually loved working nights. That wasn't it. The simple truth was that it hadn't exactly been his choice. He didn't work the night because that is what he had wanted. It was really thrust upon him. Still, Tony had come to realize that he loved working nights.

There's something different in the night, something that was never there when he worked days. The sights. The sounds. The smells. The clientele. Ha! He couldn't deny that people who were up, out, and about during the night were a different breed than those who lived their lives during the daylight hours.

People at night are changed. There is a quality about them that comes out in the dark that most people will never see in the light. But not Tony. Tony got to see all of the delicious quirkiness of night behavior. He didn't mind any of it.

Sure, the idea had been off-putting at first. He couldn't think of anyone on the job who had desired the night. He had always heard that there were some people that sought it out, but he had never met any. No, everyone he knew had been put in a similar situation to him, having it put upon them against their will. While some struggled initially, everyone came to accept it eventually.

He laughed at the memory of his first few nights. The agony. The denial. The mental fight with himself. At least he wasn't the only one. Everyone went through the same process at first. But then you settle into it. You grow to accept it. You come to love it. Eventually you get to a place where you even have a hard time remembering life before the job.

He racked his brain. How long HAD it been now? Goodness, that first encounter with his recruiter must have been 78 years ago now. Recruiter. Tony smiled to himself. It almost makes the job seem legitimate. He would hardly call it that. Still, that encounter with the vampire had forever altered the course of his life, and now the nights were his for all time. Tony sighed and looked at the moon, bright overhead.

Time to get to work . . .

48

NOTHING REALLY MATTERS

Sterile.

That was the word they used to describe examination rooms, wasn't it?

Gerald Simmons thought it was ridiculous. Sterile. It was supposed to convey the state of cleanliness in the examination room. In reality, he thought it just meant white and sparsely furnished. A counter with a sink. A trash can. A stool for the doctor to sit on. A cushioned table the nurse had called a bed.

Gerald smirked to himself. Bed. Pfft. Whatever. It was no bed he EVER wanted to sleep in. No one would. Still, he had dutifully disrobed, placed his folded clothes on the counter, and now sat on that bed in a breezy hospital gown that, even though he had tied it, never lost the feeling that it was always ready to fall off his body.

This examination room was exactly like every other one he had been in. Why was that? Was there a secret doctor cabal no one knew about where the powers that be decided exactly how everything would look and feel, no matter the doctor's specialty? He couldn't place his finger on it, but Gerald knew there was some sort of scam at play.

His therapist had called him out on these kinds of thoughts last week. What was it Dr. Larry had said? That's right – Gerald was fixating on the feelings of people being in on a scam in order to deflect from his real feelings and dealing with his situation.

He sighed. Dr. Larry was most likely right. It wasn't the doctor's fault, nor was it the fault of the examination room – although it WAS suspicious that every room always felt the same. No, the real issue was that Gerald had never expected to be spending so much time in doctors' offices and examination rooms. He had always been very careful about healthy habits and the kind of life he lived. Since he was a child, he had never cared for junk food. Give him something savory instead of sweet. As an adult, his regular diet was the stuff of the dreams of those who made food documentaries. He never deprived himself, but his version of normal was what most Americans would consider extremely, if not overly, healthy. Gerald was also an avid rower. He had crewed when he was at university and, even though he no longer lived near a body of water, his gym had some state-of-the-art rowing machines that nearly felt like the real thing. No, for all intents and purposes, Gerald was the picture of health.

There was a quick two-rap knock on the door and the doctor entered before Gerald could even respond.

"Okay, Mr. Simmons. I see that I'm the fourth specialist you've seen in the last two years. Let's talk about the spread of your cancer."

49

ONE MORE SUNRISE

When James heard the news he just had to get out of the apartment and go for a run. He didn't know how much more bad news he could endure.

"It can't last forever," his friend told him.

"But what if it does?" he moaned.

Three hundred seventy-two days ago his dad died. Dad had been his best friend his entire life. One hundred twenty-nine days ago the company he had worked for the past eight years reorganized, and he had still hadn't found a new job.

Three days ago his fiancée dumped him. The entire four years they had been together she had talked about how great it felt to have found the perfect guy and the wedding was planned. But she met someone on a business trip and . . . well . . . that's history, now.

The phone call this morning told him the test results looked bad. To come in to the doctor's office at ten a.m. for the details.

"The negativity can't last forever," his friend told him.

"But what if it does?"

As he jogged the familiar route he remembered how it felt to have everything go right. Spending time with Dad. A job he loved, making good money. The love of his life by his side.

They listened to music, went on cruises, and watched movies. They did everything together. But what struck him at this moment was the way they enjoyed getting out early to see the sunrise. Sometimes over the water. Sometimes from a mountain top. Early morning break of dawn had always symbolized the start of a new day, a new era, a new beginning. And they loved planning their life together. Every day was new, always positive, always fresh.

But that life was over.

The medical news was worse than he expected. Cancer in his left elbow? How do you get that anyway? Preliminary results indicated it had already metastasized. They could only guess how much longer he had, and recommended surgery, then chemo. First on the list was to remove his left arm. James was left-handed.

Leaving the office, he realized he had some important questions to consider. What would life look like? Did he want to go on living? Before he did anything, he wanted to experience one more sunrise.

50

PEREGRINE WENDELL SORELY

Peregrine Wendell Sorley had spent his entire adult life chasing a single, impossible dream: to visit every country that existed in the year he was born—1975. Not the world as it was now, with its shifting borders and renamed republics, but the world as it had been then, when 137 sovereign states stood on the map. Some still existed. Others—East Germany, Yugoslavia, Czechoslovakia, South Vietnam, South Yemen, the Soviet Union, Sikkim, and the Bantustans—had dissolved into history. But Peregrine insisted that if they had existed when he drew his first breath, they counted.

And if they counted, he would go.

He had visited more than 130 of them already, filling his journals with stamps, sketches, and the ritual checklists he created for each nation: traditional foods to eat, beers or liquors to sample, and a one-page language sheet with greetings, pleasantries, and essential questions. He believed that to truly visit a country, one must speak to its people in their own tongue—even if only a few phrases.

In Poland, he had charmed a grandmother selling pierogi by greeting her with a careful, *"Dzień dobry . . . Przepraszam, gdzie jest dworzec?"* She had laughed, corrected his pronunciation, and insisted he take an extra dumpling "for effort."

In Vietnam, he had ordered street food with, *"Xin chào . . . Tôi muốn gọi món ăn địa phương,"* earning a delighted clap from the vendor who served him a bowl of phở fragrant enough to make him weep.

In Yemen—well, Yemen was still ahead of him. And Yemen was where the trouble would begin.

The remaining countries on his list were the ones the U.S. Department of State advised avoiding entirely. Places where governments had fractured, militias controlled the roads, and a single wrong turn could end a life. But Peregrine was running out of time. He was fifty-one now, and the world was not becoming safer.

The philosophical problem of the "vanished nations" haunted him almost as much as the danger. What did it truly mean to visit a country that no longer existed? Was standing in Berlin enough to count as East Germany, or was that merely a convenient fiction? Should he have gone to Leipzig instead, where the GDR still lingered in architecture and societal memory? When he visited Belgrade, did that count for Yugoslavia, or should he have crossed into Sarajevo, Skopje, or Ljubljana to honor the full breadth of what once was? Eventually, he created a rubric—his attempt to impose order on a world that refused to stay still:

- Visit the former capital
- Eat a traditional dish from the era

- Speak to someone who lived under the old flag

It wasn't perfect, but it was honest. And honesty mattered to him more than safety.

Which was why he now found himself in the back of a battered Toyota Hilux, bouncing across the desert toward the outskirts of Ma'rib, Yemen, clutching his notebook of checklists like a talisman.

His fixer, a wiry man named Samir, drove with one hand and smoked with the other. "You understand," Samir said, "that if we are stopped, I will say I do not know you."

Peregrine nodded. "I wouldn't expect otherwise."

"You have your phrases?"

He flipped open his language sheet. "*As-salāmu ʿalaykum . . . Ayna al-ḥammām?*" He smiled. "And the more important one: *Ana musāfir . . . urīdu an azūr baladakum.*"

Samir snorted. "If they shoot at us, no phrase will help."

The first checkpoint appeared as a cluster of sandbags and a rusted oil drum. Armed men stepped into the road. Peregrine felt his pulse thrum in his throat. Samir muttered something under his breath, slowed the truck, and rolled down the window.

A man with a rifle leaned in. "Where are you going?"

Peregrine spoke before Samir could answer. "*Ana musāfir . . . urīdu an azūr baladakum.*"

The man blinked, surprised. Then he laughed a short, sharp bark. "A tourist? Here?" He waved them through. "Go. But do not stay long."

Samir exhaled shakily as they drove on. "You are insane," he said. "But lucky."

In Ma'rib, Peregrine completed his ritual with quiet reverence. He ate saltah, the bubbling, herb-scented stew served in a hot stone bowl. He sampled a thimble of araq, the anise liquor that burned pleasantly down his throat. He spoke with an elderly shopkeeper who had lived through the days of South Yemen, checking off the final requirement for a defunct state.

For a moment, he felt triumphant. Yemen was nearly complete. Only two more countries remained.

Then the gunfire started.

It came from the west—sharp, echoing cracks that sent people scattering in every direction. Samir grabbed Peregrine's arm. "We must go. Now."

They ran through narrow alleys as dust rose around them. A shell exploded somewhere nearby, rattling windows and sending a tremor through the ground beneath their feet. Peregrine stumbled, clutching his notebook. He could not lose it. It held every country, every checklist, every phrase he had ever learned.

They reached the truck just as a second explosion rocked the street. Samir shoved him inside. "Hold on."

They sped through the city, weaving around debris. Smoke curled into the sky in dark, twisting plumes. Peregrine felt the weight of his dream pressing on him—not as inspiration, but as a question. Was this worth dying for? Was any list worth this?

A third explosion hit close enough to lift the truck off its wheels. They slammed back to the ground. Samir cursed, fighting the steering wheel. "We cannot stay on this road!"

Peregrine's ears rang. His vision blurred. He tasted dust and metal.

Another burst of gunfire shredded the air.

Samir shouted something he couldn't hear.

The truck skidded sideways, tires screaming against the broken pavement.

Peregrine's notebook slipped from his hands, its pages fluttering like wounded birds.

He reached for it.

The world went white.

Then—

Silence.

A ringing, distant and hollow.

He felt himself lying on his side, half-buried in sand. Smoke drifted overhead in thin, wavering ribbons. The truck was overturned. Samir was nowhere in sight.

Peregrine tried to move. Pain lanced through his ribs, sharp enough to steal his breath. He tasted blood.

His notebook lay a few feet away, open to his Yemen page. The checklist was nearly complete. Only one box remained unchecked.

He crawled toward it, inch by inch.

A shadow fell across him.

Boots. Several pairs.

Voices speaking Arabic he couldn't quite make out.

He forced out a phrase, barely a whisper. "*As-salāmu . . . 'alaykum . . .*"

The boots moved closer.

A rifle clicked.

Peregrine reached for his notebook.

The world narrowed to a single breath.

And then—

Nothing.

51

PIERCING EYES

The mirror never lied.

All of her bad decisions stared right back at her.

There were the obvious ones like consistently bad dietary choice, and only less obvious like the baggy eyes from all night bingers and poor sleep.

But there were also the non-obvious ones—the ones deep inside from the depression and self-loathing that moved inside her and drove her to some dark thoughts about self-harm.

She usually wore a subtle smile and avoided eye contact. Put up a strong front and cheerfully returned greetings and "how are yous."

But the mirror never lied.

52

PIZZA

The summer of 1975 in Minneapolis was warm but not hot. But the temperature in Darren's car was rising as he kept driving around town. Forty-seven minutes into this delivery, he was completely lost. He'd only been working at the Big Beau's Pizza Parlor for 3 months and the boss finally let him do his first delivery. He'd spent the last ninety days learning about making pizza and how to take orders, write receipts, and manage the inventory. Beau made his employees do everything in the store before he allowed them to do deliveries and represent his life's work out in town with customers.

Darren was driving his dad's 1961 Dodge which he realized was probably sucking down all of the money he made from his job just to fill up the gas tank. And now he was on the far side of town and had no idea how to get to the address scribbled on the piece of paper sitting next to him on the seat. The sun was starting to set.

He would have given up already but he didn't know how to get back to the pizza shop or even how to get home. He was completely and utterly lost.

"I'm definitely going to get fired," he thought.

Then up ahead he saw a glimmer of a light from a farm house.

"Whew, maybe I can stop there and call for help."

He parked the car and knocked on the door.

A weathered old woman opened it inward.

"Can I help you, young man?"

"Yes ma'am, could I possibly come inside and use your phone? I'm lost and need to call my boss or my dad to figure out how to get home."

"Oh no! come on in, young fella."

As he stepped inside a huge flash of light blinded them both.

Hummmmmmmmmmmmm. A loud metallic buzzing filled the air.

And then Darren looked up into the sky at the light. A giant football shaped object floated in the sky. The old lady gasped. "It's the Germans in a zeppelin!"

"Ma'am, I don't think that's Germans. I think it's… it's… it's ALIENS!"

Suddenly a greenish blue light beam shone down from the spaceship directly on Darren's dad's car. Then the light slowly started moving towards Darren and the old lady. They were both too shocked to move and then the light got to them and they were literally frozen still. They couldn't move even if they wanted to. A hole opened on the ship and what looked like a rope or a pole lowered to the ground. A small creature slid down to the ground. It looked like a cross between a man and the teddy bear Darren's little sister carried around all the time. It couldn't have been more than

2 feet tall. As Darren and the old woman stood immobilized by the light ray, the little bear/man kind of skip/hop/pranced to the door of the car. He smiled with glee as he sniffed the air. He pulled out a little wand and waved it at the car. The door opened. The little guy disappeared into the car and popped right back out again carrying the pizza Darren was supposed to deliver!

"Hey that's not yours! I need to deliver that or I'm gonna get fired!"

The bear/man looked at Darren and mumbled something in what must have been his native language. Then he turned and scampered back to the rope/pole, grabbed it, and it zipped back up into the spaceship. In the blink of an eye the ship disappeared into the sky and Darren and the old woman were left on the front porch speechless.

Darren looked at the old woman. The woman looked at Darren.

"So can I use your phone?"

53

Q & A

"May I ask you a question?"
"Sounds important?"
"There are some very famous questions, you know."
"Give me an example?"
"Let's see if I can name a few."

To be or not to be?
Where's Waldo?
What's the meaning of life?
Et tu, Bruté?
Where in the world is the poky little puppy?
Wherefore art thou Romeo?
Who ya gonna call?
If I had another face, do you think I would wear this one?"
What would it profit a man to gain the whole world but lose his soul?

"Why are you suddenly so interested in questions?"
"Like I said, I have a question for you?"
"Sounds serious. What is it?"
"Will you marry me?"

54

THE QUESTION

Are we there yet?
No.
Are we there yet?
No.
Are we there yet?
No.
Are we there yet?
No.
Are we there yet?
No.
Are we there yet?
No.
Are we there yet?
No.
Are we there yet?
No.
Are we there yet?
No.

Are we there yet?
No.
Are we there yet?
No.

55

A QUIET ROUTINE

Elliot was a good husband, a dedicated worker, and a quietly devout Christian. After a short tour of service in the Air Force as a Human Resources Specialist, he used the GI Bill to attend college. While earning a liberal arts degree, he met and married Martha, and after graduating, he joined the Bureau of Prisons as a Human Resources Officer.

Sixteen years had passed, and very little in his life had changed. Martha still taught 2nd Grade at Lincoln Elementary. She'd already watched her first five classes graduate, and one of her former students had even returned last year as its newest hire, teaching 4th Grade.

St. Peters, MO was by no means a small town. A suburb of St. Louis with over 58,000 people, it ranked among Missouri's largest cities. But that wasn't the Lincoln Elementary where Martha worked. She and Elliot lived in Troy, MO—Lincoln County's seat and a quiet exurb about an hour outside of St. Louis.

Troy was a much smaller town with about 12,000 people, but the semi-rural rhythm suited Elliot and Martha just fine. Elliot's only complaint was the hour-long commute each way to the Bureau facility in the Gateway to the West, though books on tape softened the grind.

After years of trying for children of their own, Martha and Elliot finally sought testing. It wasn't just one of them: Martha's womb was inhospitable, and Elliot's count was low. Children weren't in their future, but nothing dimmed the devotion and warmth they shared.

They were financially stable, happily married, content in their work, and grateful for the pleasant life they'd built.

Now, sixteen years in, Elliot realized he hadn't really done anything just for himself since college. The quiet routine wasn't bad, but it had begun to feel stale. Frankly, he was bored.

His 9-5 job at the Bureau meant he usually got home at 6:04 p.m. Sometimes it was closer to 6:00 or 6:10. Most days, he returned to find Martha grading, massaging lesson plans, or preparing crafts, but this week was parent teacher conferences. She wouldn't be home for another hour.

He sat at the office computer, opened up Chrome, and typed a query.

"top classes to learn new skills in st louis missouri"

AI suggested hands-on art workshops at Craft Alliance, or taking a class at St. Louis Community College (STLCC) in culinary arts, dance, or photography. A top Yelp result highlighted local glass-blowing studios, and the search result from STLCC's own site promoted its "Personal Enrichment Classes." Elliot clicked the link, curious to discover what inspires him.

"So many options . . . hmm . . . "

The familiar click-clack of the dead-bold and long creeeeeaaak of the front door signaled Martha's arrival.

"Good evening, honey," Elliot bellowed in stentorian fashion. "I'm in the office."

Martha scooted across the living room, set her things down on the table, then stepped into the office. She gently place her hand on Elliot's shoulder, leaned in, and gave him a tender kiss.

"I love you."

"After sixteen years, I still get chills hearing you say that. How were the parent-teacher meetings?"

"I hate to say it, even 2nd Grader parents seem more entitled each year. Where is all the cordiality and involvement that parents used to show? I swear there was one couple that I've never even seen before. I thought it was Julie's mom that always picks her up, but it turns out it's her older sister. I didn't even know."

"Well, they're lucky to have you. Best teacher in the state."

"Thank you. And you? How was your day?"

"It was good."

Staring intently and waiting for more, but too tired to coax it out of him, Martha let it go. Intending to wash up and throw together a chicken salad for dinner, Elliot stopped her.

"Hey . . . I was thinking I might take a class at the community college."

"Oh yeah? St Louis Community College? What would you take?"

" I don't really know." He pointed at the screen. "What do you think?"

Martha picked up her glasses from where they hung on her sweater and seated them on the end of her nose. "Huhh

. . . . Photography could be fun. You've always taken great pictures when we're out. Maybe you could do something with that?"

"Photography, huh? Yeah . . . that could be fun."

Elliot let the idea settle. It wasn't just a hobby; it felt like a small doorway opening somewhere inside him. He couldn't remember the last time something new had sparked even a flicker of excitement. Most days were predictable—comforting, yes, but predictable in a way that had slowly dulled the edges of his own curiosity.

Martha watched him, her expression softening. "You know," she said, "you've always had an eye for things. Little details. Moments other people miss."

He glanced at her, surprised by the warmth in her voice. "You really think so?"

"I do." She squeezed his shoulder. "Maybe it's time you did something that's just for you."

The words landed deftly, yet with a certain weightiness, nevertheless. He realized how long it had been since he'd allowed himself to want something—not for practicality, not for stability, not because it fit neatly into the life they'd built, but simply because it made him feel alive.

He turned back to the screen. The photography course description mentioned weekend outings, learning to work with natural light, capturing motion, telling stories through images. He imagined himself outside on a crisp morning, camera in hand, noticing the world again. Noticing himself again.

A tinge of excitement spread through his chest.

"You know," he said, "I think I'd like that. Maybe I could even take some pictures of your classroom. Or the fall festival. Something fun."

Martha smiled, the tiredness in her eyes easing. "I'd love that. And I think you will too."

He clicked the "Register" button before he could overthink it. A small, almost imperceptible thrill ran through him—like the first breath after stepping outside on a bright day.

For the first time in a long while, Elliot felt something shift. Not a dramatic upheaval, not a grand revelation—just a quiet, steady sense of forward motion. A reminder that life still held corners he hadn't explored, skills he hadn't tried, ways of seeing he hadn't yet learned.

Maybe the routine wasn't the problem. Maybe he'd simply forgotten to look up.

And now, with a camera soon in his hands, he would.

56

QUITTERS NEVER PROSPER

This wasn't the first time the young couple had quarreled over the matter. Picking up in the middle of a tense engagement, the intensity has escalated higher than normal, and instead of shutting down and retreating into herself, she digs in sticks to her guns.

[F] "You said you were gonna quit!"

[M] "And I DID quit! But a lotta good that did me! Not like you were any help in the matter anyway!"

[F] "All I been try'na do it is take care of you. You gon' go get yo'self killed and leave this family high and dry!"

[M] "All I do, I do for this family! There's no break to be had, and it ain't easy out there."

[M] *Hanging his head in desperation*

[F] *Approaching matter-of-factly with a stern look*

[M] *Looking up to make eye contact without really raising his head*

[F] *Pausing mid-step and starting to reach out, before continuing to him and putting her arms around his neck*

[F] "We appreciate you. We really do. We just love you too much to see you go . . . You said you'd quit."

[M] "I will. I really will."

57

A REAL MAN

Andrew and Sara met at the mall food court on Saturday afternoon a few weeks before Christmas and both knew right away it was love at first sight. He moved into her apartment three days later and everything was great. Sara felt like the luckiest woman in the world to have found true love at age twenty-three.

Two days before Christmas, Adam told her he had invited a few friends over to celebrate.

"Wait a minute," she said. "You never talked to me about that."

"Well, I'm telling you now."

"It doesn't work that way, Adam. You ought to have the courtesy to talk to me before bringing people into my home."

"Hey, I'm the man here. I make the decisions."

When Sara disagreed, the discussion grew into an argument and Adam hit her and cursed.

"This isn't what love looks like," she blurted out.

He grabbed her by the arm, spun her around, and sneered into her face. "Well then, what do you think love looks like?"

"Love is patient and kind. Love is mutual respect, being there to serve each other, and help each other. But never forcing or imposing your will and demanding things go your way."

"You're kidding, right?"

"No, I'm not. If you don't know the basics about love, it was a tragic mistake to fall in love with you and ask you to move in."

Adam pushed her to the floor.

"And one more thing. Love never hits, hurts, insults, or disrespects." By now, Sara was crying.

He kicked her in the back and spat at her. Then he grabbed his jacket and keys and drove away.

Sara got up from the floor and drove to urgent care for an exam and then to the police station to file a report. The officer urged her to go to the county building and request a restraining order. After doing that, she needed time to think and sort things out so she went to her favorite restaurant, requested a booth in the back and ordered a club sandwich and a vanilla shake—her favorite comfort food.

As she was sitting there eating and thinking, Adam walked in and approached her.

"I've been following you all afternoon. Now get in the car. We're going home," he demanded.

"You don't live there anymore."

He grabbed her by the hair and began pulling her towards the exit when a man stepped in front of him and told him to let go of her.

"Get out of my way," Adam shouted.

"Dude if you think this how love works, you are sadly mistaken."

"So tell me, then. How does love work?" Adam snarled at the stranger who was an inch or so shorter. If it came down to a fight, he was sure he would win.

"Look, pal. Love is gentle and faithful. Love doesn't selfishly demand its own way. Love always honors the one you say you love. It's not being a bully or a tough guy. So I'm telling you one last time to let her go."

Adam let go of Sara's hair and took a swing at the stranger, who blocked the punch, grasped Adam's wrist, twisted the arm behind Adam's back, and used his leg in a sweeping motion to take Adam to the floor face down, his knee pressed firmly on Adam's back.

"One more thing," the stranger added. "Love protects and defends, it does not attack. A real man knows this, so obviously, you aren't a real man."

While holding Adam down on the floor, the stranger pulled out his phone, dialed 9-1-1, and asked for the police to come to the restaurant. A patrol car was in the area and got there pretty fast. The restaurant employees and the dozen or so customers all gave the same eye witness report, and Adam was arrested.

The stranger walked over to Sara.

"Hi. I'm Andrew. Friends call me Drew. Are you OK?"

"Yes, thank you for stepping in when you did."

"You're welcome. Can I do anything else for you?"

"I can't think of anything."

"Well, here's my phone number if you ever need help or if you ever wanna talk. The police won't hold him very long. They'll ask you if you want to press charges. If you do, it might take a while for it to be settled, and you might be in danger, depending on what he decides to do, so be careful."

58

RELEARNING TO FEEL

Suzanne was a clinical psychiatrist. What she lacked in warmth and presence at home, she compensated for with unwavering dedication to her patients. Some might call her an absentee mother, but after she discovered Bill with his secretary in their home, she withdrew mentally and emotionally.

The divorce was quick and clean. Both were successful professionals, and money was never an issue. She kept the house; he kept the Mercedes and the boat. Their ten-year-old son, Richard, was sent to boarding school—minimizing the immediate impact, though he would eventually return to live with Suzanne.

Summer arrived quietly, its sweltering heat discouraging any outdoor activity. Yet the emotionally cold home was no place for a boy. Suzanne and Richard showed little interest in being there; but at ten, what choice did he have? The distance between them stemmed largely from

Richard's striking resemblance to his father, and it was a constant reminder of the betrayal and pain. Inside, she was dying of grief; outwardly, she appeared dull and apathetic.

Richard, once the dutiful child carrying the burdens of upper-middle-class expectations, began to lash out. His explosive outbursts, no matter the setting, brought Suzanne shame. In response, she prescribed a cocktail of Prozac, Cymbalta, and Elavil. Perhaps it was well-meaning, but it fit her pattern: lean on work, disengage from family. The medications blunted his emotions, leaving Richard a mellowed, sedated shell of a child—chemically incapable of feeling anything deeply.

Seven years slipped by.

Richard—now Ricky—was alive, but not truly living.

He could think, converse, and navigate social encounters, but without emotions, life merely happened to him. Until he met Rose.

Rose embodied everything Ricky was not. She was free-thinking, free-living, and free loving, unhampered by the societal constraints that defined Ricky's world. They crossed paths by happenstance the summer before Ricky was supposed to go off to Yale.

Unlike anyone he had ever known, Ricky fell hard for Rose; as hard as someone strung out on a cocktail of psych meds could. She invited him to go camping with her and some of her friends. At the start of the trip, she tossed his meds. For the first time in seven years, Ricky began to feel.

It was terrible. Sad. Devastating. Years of numbness had buried his lost childhood and the pain of parental neglect. Yet the very fact that he was feeling—anything—was extraordinary.

Ricky also felt joy for the first in recent memory. He smiled. He even laughed. A week and a half with Rose and her friends let sunlight into Ricky's soul, dangling a fragile hope that he might truly live again.

When he returned, Suzanne was waiting, and she did not look happy.

"I called, and I messaged you. Where have you been?"

"Mom . . . we need to talk."

"Don't you try to turn this around on me."

"Mom. Shut the f#$% up, and actually listen to me."

Suzanne paled, her eyes widening as Richard's words hit her with the force of seven silent years. She stood frozen—mute, statue-still—unable to reconcile the boy she had numbed into compliance with the young man now staring her down.

"Mom," he said, voice steady but trembling at the edges. "You left me to be raised by the staff, by the school—by anyone but you. What Dad did to you . . . to us . . . it was awful. But it wasn't an excuse to erase me. I'm your son. I deserved more than the scraps you had left."

Her lips parted, but no sound came.

"You pour everything into your patients," he continued, "and nothing into me. It's not too late for us to be a family. But things have to change. *You* have to change. And we're starting right now."

He stepped forward and wrapped his arms around her.

For a heartbeat, she remained rigid. Then her breath broke—shattered—and a single tear slid down her cheek. Another followed. And then the dam burst. Years of grief, betrayal, guilt, and self-loathing poured out of her in shaking sobs. She clung to him as if he were the only solid thing left in her collapsing world.

"I'm sorry," she choked out. "Richard . . . I'm so, so sorry."

He pulled back just enough to meet her eyes. "It's Ricky now."

She nodded, the smallest, most fragile gesture of acceptance she had ever made.

He held her shoulders, steadying her. "I'm giving us one chance. Don't waste it."

Suzanne swallowed hard, tears still streaming. "I won't," she whispered. "I swear I won't."

And for the first time in years, they stood together—not as a ghost of a family, not as two people orbiting the same house, but as a mother and son taking their first, trembling step toward something new.

59

THE RIDDLE

Emily just knew it had to be in his library, and she wasn't about to give up just because she hadn't figured it out yet.

"Uncle Cecil and I spent so many hours together in here. It was our favorite place to hang out. We talked. He told me stories. We had lunch in here. He showed me pictures and books and souvenirs from his travels around the world. I practically grew up in here. So, when he died without a will, I knew there would be a note somewhere. I just didn't know it would be a riddle.

"Read it to me again, Emily."

"Okay."

The finder of the key is the person who
Understands the radius of the earth times two
Travel east from this very spot
If you want to have a shot
Look straight down onto the ground
And the answer will be found

"But Emily, the experts have dissected the riddle. They know that the radius of the earth is about 3,959 miles, depending on where you measure and whose numbers you're using. But that's the distance your uncle used in his lectures. When you double that, it comes to 7,918 miles. And exactly 7,918 miles east from here is in the ocean, about five hundred miles east of Japan. There's nothing there. Not even a tiny island. Which means there is nothing to the riddle. It's a red herring or a smokescreen." Geoffery was running out of patience.

"No! I know him. I understand that the police might not get it, but I believe Uncle Cecil wrote it for me, and for me only. He knows me and he knows that I know him and how he thinks."

After reading the note again, Emily was certain that the answer to his riddle had to be here in this room.

"But we've looked a dozen times," Geoffery reminded her. "So have the police. You've racked your brain over and over, trying to come up with it. Maybe there isn't an answer. Maybe it's just too hard. Too hard for the police detectives working the case, and too hard for you and me."

"Maybe we're trying too hard. What if it's a lot simpler, so simple that I'm looking past the solution?"

"Well, I'm going outside to get some fresh air. I have nothing more to offer."

Geoffery and Emily were pretty good as secret agents, but this kind of investigation was different. She wondered if maybe it wasn't detective work or spy techniques that this called for. Instead, it called for something else, something personal. That's it! It required knowing Uncle Cecil personally and knowing his history. Maybe even having a shared history. Could that be it?

Emily sat in the chair behind her uncle's desk. Professor Cecil Underwood, world class historian and traveler. Where would he have hidden the key?

As she sat there looking around the library, her eyes watering, so many memories flooded her mind. So many shared experiences. She looked at the floor-to-ceiling shelving. The art and mementos on the walls, the shelves, and the counters. The books, the papers, the maps, the parquet floor, the antique wooden globe that she used to spin when she was a little girl. Her mother always told her to stop spinning the globe, but Uncle Cecil just winked and when her mother wasn't in the room, said it was okay to do it.

The globe? Maybe the riddle referred to that globe instead of the earth. She took her uncle's measuring tape from the drawer and went over to the globe. She measured the circumference, the diameter, and the radius. The radius was exactly 20 inches. 20 inches times two would be 40 inches. Which way was east? Knowing where he stored his compass, she retrieved it and returned to the globe. She pulled out the tape to 40 inches and lay it straight towards the east and set it onto the floor.

"Aha! There it is!"

Etched into the wooden floor in a manner that blended into the parquetry, was the phrase *Emily's favorite spot*.

She had never told anyone about her favorite spot. Only Cecil knew about it. She ran over to the far corner of the room and opened the lower cabinet door. She used to hide in there when she was three and four and had confided to Uncle Cecil that it was her favorite spot. She looked inside. Taped to the under side of the shelf was a key. A key that she recognized.

She took the key back to the globe, spun it around for old times' sake, then located the slot on the equator in Indonesia, inserted the key, and turned it.

60

ROMINA AND JULIO

It was Julio's Junior Year at UC Berkely, and he was at the top of his class in the undergraduate Business Management program. Straight As, and a passion to see the world, he knew before the end of his freshman year that he wanted to do the IES Abroad program in Milan. Despite growing up in Chula Vista and speaking Spanish as the primary language in his home, Julio opted to take Italian for his mandatory language credit. 9th grade was Italian 1-2, and he fell in love with Italy and everything about it, even if all of his hermanas, primos, y primas teased him for being a cultural traitor.

* * *

Abofazl Ahmedi and his new bride Fatemeh migrated from Tehran to the outskirts of Rome in 1993. They were part of a burgeoning diaspora, even though Italy wasn't a common destination for other Persians. Romina was born a few years later, and the cost of living in Rome became a little too preclusive to remain, even with a regular salary in the import/export business. The Ahmedi's moved to the province of Lodi. In the Lombardy region, it was essentially an exurb of Milan, a mere 30 minutes away. To call Abofazl and Fatemeh a beautiful couple would be an understatement, but even from a young age, Romina turned heads everywhere she went.

* * *

His sophomore year of High School, Julio took Italian 3-4. His Junior year, he took Italian 5-6. Leave it to Bonita Vista HS to have one of the most robust offerings of foreign languages across San Diego County (and probably most of the US). Julio excelled at math, but had to work at science. His hard work, discipline, and forward thinking rewarded him with a near-perfect, unweighted GPA of 3.99, an International Baccalaureate diploma, and multiple AP and honors classes to his credit. He was the captain of the wrestling team his Junior and Senior years and regularly delivered food for the Catholic Charities community outreach program. His natural intellectual curiosity and proclivities to being a genuinely good person that cared about his community paid off, and his was one of the 18% of applications that UC Berkeley accepted in 2017—up from the typical 12%, but still extremely selective.

* * *

From the ages of 18 to 23, Romina worked in the hospitality and tourism industry. A huge step up from how models are treated (an industry that repeatedly came knocking on her door), her stunning looks did much to make her everyone's favorite concierge. At 23, she wanted a change and became a "badanti," looking after an elderly woman in Milan as a live-in caregiver. Milan was her absolute favorite and the fashion hub of Italy. There was never a shortage of beautiful dresses to admire along the Via Monte Napoleone and Via della Spiga. Sure, she couldn't afford any of them, but the reflections in the window literally allowed her to see herself in them.

* * *

Julio thought the Duomo di Milano was a pastiche of the Notre Dame (de Paris) and St. Stephen's Cathedral in Vienna. One of his first priorities after arriving in Milan mid-January of 2020 was to see all of Europe's capitals. He went to one every other weekend, utilizing trans-European trains and the public transportation within each city. He wasn't saving a single cent, but when would he ever get to be in Europe again?

Paris, Vienna, Berlin, and of course, Rome. Not too shabby for only having lived in Europe a couple of months. He spent the in-between-travel weekends exploring Milan and enjoyed it at least as much as the international travel. Italy held a special place in his heart.

Then entry in his journal read: "March 7th, 2020. I just visited the Quadrilatero della Moda (the fashion quadrilateral). They wouldn't even let me go into the stores because apparently I look like a poor college student (FACTS). My life will never be the same. She was "gorgeous," and that word fails to do her justice. I don't think my jaw literally dropped, but I know I stopped and ogled for a moment. Just… wow."

He couldn't help but go back to the Café delle Colonne, whence he first saw her. With no other leads and no idea how else to see her again, Julio arrived as the café was opening, and plopped himself down streetside with a clear vantage of the avenue. His phone was fully charged, his book was neatly preserved and uncreased with more than half of it to go, and he planned to spend minimal time looking at either.

* * *

Romina was used to people gawking at her. It came par for the course as the most beautiful Front-of-House worker on the continent. In fact, it was a large motivator for her to change professions. Nevertheless, she could shirk off the slack-jawed gazes with ease.

* * *

Julio, despite his best efforts, couldn't take his eyes off her. There she was again! He couldn't believe his plan worked. If only he'd kept planning beyond the idea of how to see her again.

"Sometimes you can over-plan these things." The quotation from Dusty Bottoms in Three Amigos came to mind, perfectly fitting the situation in which he found himself.

He had nothing.

* * *

Just because Romina dismissed the gazes didn't mean she was oblivious to the onlookers. She recognized Julio from the day before, and he had the same, magnificent, brightness and intensity in his eyes. It wasn't the typical, seedy, down-dressing she so loathed . . . it was a vivid, vibrant soul reaching out and connecting with hers.

He wasn't looking at her body, not that he didn't want to. He was peering straight into her soul.

Romina redirected and instead of walking right past him, aimed straight for the chair across the small bistro-table along the avenue. She sat down and they locked eyes for a fleeting moment that felt like eternity.

* * *

A full minute and a half later, realizing that he wasn't dreaming despite staring off into her eyes, Julio became momentarily self-conscious and struggled with what to say. Three years of Italian classes in high school, another year of collegiate coursework, and a month in country, but he couldn't find the words.

* * *

Romina did the talking for him. Introducing herself, talking a little about what she was doing, and quickly wrapping it up so she could get back to Signora Francesca, a sweet Italian lady.

* * *

Taken aback about Romina describing herself as a "Bandita" about to go rob a poor octogenarian, Julio's face noticeably changed.

Previously dumbfounded, Julio spit out the perfect Italian he'd worked nearly half his life to develop.

"Hai appena detto che sei un bandita in procinto di derubare la vedova di una contessa italiana?" (In other words, "Did you just say you are a bandit about to go rob a widowed Italian countess?")

* * *

"Cosa!? Certo che no!" Romina couldn't believe the accusation.

* * *

"Bandita?!"

* * *

Putting her face in her palms to try stifling the heartfelt laugh and unable to prevent a related snort while guffawing, Romina corrected him.

"No. Non sono una bandita. Sono un assistente. Sono un assistente convivente."

* * *

Julio's cheeks lit up like a peony in full bloom, ablaze with a hue of crimson reserved for the most severe of embarrassment.

* * *

They exchanged numbers and agreed to meet again tomorrow an hour earlier so they could talk.

* * *

The entire country shut down the next day. The region of Lombardy, together with fourteen additional northern and central provinces, went on quarantine due to SARS-Cov2, also known as COVID-19. They were on lock-down.

Their love was blooming, the attraction undeniable, and their contact forbidden.

61

RUMORS

At 6'4" and 280 pounds, Victor stood out like a sore thumb in his freshman English class. Even though he was soft-spoken and gentle, most people kept their distance, but they stared. That was inevitable in the ninth grade. They talked about him. That, too, was unavoidable. But mostly they avoided him, which led to a lonely existence, for him.

There are unkind people everywhere, bullies all around the world, and one in particular decided his mission in life was to hurt Victor. Bruce started with insults and name-calling, and subsequently transitioned to taunting. Victor remained calm.

Then came the rumors about Victor and his family, followed by outright lies, fabrication of details that simply weren't true, all designed to get under Victor's skin, but he didn't respond the way Bruce wanted him to. Then came the challenge.

In front of about forty students in the quad outside the cafeteria, Bruce cursed at Victor, insulted his family, called him the stupidest person in the whole school, and told him to get ready for the worst beating he could imagine. Victor turned to Bruce, and for the first time since anybody could remember, Victor spoke.

"Bruce, I know who you are, where you come from, what your circumstances are, and I know what you're trying to do. Do you really want this show-down here in front of everybody?"

"You think you know me, huh. Okay smart guy. Give me my life story."

"Your dad's an unemployed alcoholic who is abusive to your mom and you and your sister. You live in a pretty rough part of town in a run-down house which is why you never have friends over. You're really good at basketball, but you're afraid of failure so you won't even try out for the team. You're smart, but you won't study, so you get bad grades so you can fit in with your friends. You like to intimidate people or beat them up because that makes you feel like a somebody. You like animals and are interested in becoming a veterinarian when you grow up, but your dad makes fun of you and discourages you. Shall I keep going?"

As Victor spoke, Bruce's face was turning redder. He rushed at Victor, arms flailing, curses spewing, tears flowing. Victor deflected the first two swings, spun Bruce around, pulled him into himself, and embraced him so tightly that Bruce could hardly breathe, his arms were pinned to his sides, and his face smashed up against Victor's chest. Bruce squirmed and tried to free himself but couldn't. He was trapped. Immobilized. Powerless.

"Bruce, we could be friends, you know. Being mean isn't the only kind of power. There's physical power, emotional power, intellectual power, and spiritual power. That's what I learned at my church's martial arts program. And the greatest power is love."

Bruce looked up at Victor. Then he closed his eyes, relaxed, and sobbed. Victor held him like that for a long time as the other students gawked and then slowly walked away.

When Bruce finished crying, he opened his eyes and asked, "How did you know all that about me?"

"People talk, Bruce. They talk about you, about me, about everyone. Especially when they think nobody else is listening. Plus, I have the advantage of being multilingual so they think I don't understand. So I've heard a lot about you. And I hurt for you. You have so much to offer."

"Victor, I don't have a real friend. Would you . . ."

He didn't have to finish the question. Victor released him and held out his hand.

62

SEEDS OF DISSENT

In the year 2242, humanity finally achieved a utopia of perfect efficiency. Every aspect of life was optimized, streamlined, and stripped of unnecessary frivolity. And nowhere was this more apparent than at mealtime. Food, once a source of pleasure and culture, was now a mere matter of functional nutrient delivery. The daily ration for every citizen of the gleaming Global Collective was a flavorless, beige paste called "Nutri-Slurry," dispensed from chrome spigots in every home. It contained all the necessary vitamins, minerals, and macronutrients to sustain a productive life. It was clean. It was logical. And for those that knew what food could be, it was unbearably, soul-crushingly bland.

But in the forgotten corners and shadowed alleys of the pristine metropolis, a rebellion was simmering. A revolution against the literally tasteless society. They called themselves "the Foodies" and were a small, clandestine group of individuals who risked everything for the simple pleasure of a good meal.

Their leader was a man named Jean-Luc, a descendant of a long line of French chefs. His face, usually creased with worry, would light up with an almost holy fervor when he spoke of the "Before Times," a mythical era when food was not just fuel, but an art form. His second-in-command was a woman named Paloma, a fiery Latina whose ancestors had been masters of spice and seasoning. Together, they led a motley crew of flavor-worshippers who scrounged for ancient cookbooks, cultivated illegal herb gardens on hidden rooftops and secret rooms with specialized lights, and bartered for contraband ingredients on the black market.

One evening, while the Foodies gathered in their secret hideout beneath a decommissioned nutrient processing plant, the air was thick with the forbidden aromas of garlic, onion, and roasting meat. It was a stark contrast to the sterile, ozonic atmosphere of the city above. Tonight was a special occasion. Jean-Luc had managed to procure a whole chicken, a creature so rare it was spoken of in hushed, reverent tones.

"Mes amis!" Jean-Luc proclaimed triumphantly, his voice trembling with emotion as he held up the plump, pale bird. "Tomorrow will linger in the nostrils and tastebuds of generations to come. We may not all return to gather again. But tonight, we feast!"

A respectful silence fell over the group as Jean-Luc began to prepare the chicken with the precision of a surgeon. He rubbed it with a mixture of salt, pepper, and a precious pinch of dried rosemary from Paloma's rooftop garden. He stuffed its cavity with a lemon, a small, wrinkled orb that had cost them a week's worth of energy credits.

As the bird roasted in a makeshift oven fashioned from an old incinerator unit, the Foodies prepared the side dishes. There were potatoes, smuggled from a rogue agricultural zone, roasted with garlic and thyme. There were carrots, glazed with a precious spoonful of honey. And there was wine: a dark, rich liquid fermented from stolen grapes. The Efficiency Enforcers had classified the beverage as a Schedule-A controlled substance, illegal in the highest order.

The meal was a symphony of flavors, a riot of sensations that stood in defiant opposition to the bland monotony of their daily lives. The chicken was juicy and succulent, its skin crispy and golden. The potatoes were fluffy and garlicky, the carrots sweet and tender. The wine was bold and complex, a warm caress on the palate. And for the first time in a long time, the Foodies felt truly alive.

But their celebration was short-lived. A sudden, loud banging on the steel door of their hideout sent a jolt of fear through the group.

"Efficiency Enforcers!" a voice boomed from the other side. "Open up!"

Panic erupted. The Foodies scrambled to hide the evidence of their illicit feast, but it was too late. The door burst open, and a squad of glossy, white-clad Enforcers stormed in, their faces grim and impassive.

At the head of the squad was a man named Silas, a high-ranking official in the Department of Nutritional Compliance. He surveyed the scene with a look of cold disdain, his anterior naris twitching at the unfamiliar, offending smells.

"What is the meaning of this?" Silas demanded, his voice bereft of emotion and smacking of the world he represented. "Unauthorized congregation. Consumption of non-sanctioned foodstuffs. This is a serious breach of Collective law."

Jean-Luc stepped forward, his heart pounding in his chest. "We meant no harm, sir," he said, his voice surprisingly steady. "We were just... remembering."

Silas raised an eyebrow. "Remembering what?"

"Remembering what it means to be human," Jean-Luc replied, a newfound courage welling within him. "To taste, to savor, to share a meal with friends. To find joy in something more than the pursuit of eliminating everything inconsequential and unproductive."

Silas was about to retort with a pre-programmed lecture on the virtues of nutritional optimization when a small, timid woman from the back of the group, holding a plate with a single, perfectly roasted potato, approached him.

"Would . . . would you like to try some?" she asked, her voice barely a whisper.

Silas scoffed. "I have no need for your primitive... sustenance."

But the woman persisted, her eyes pleading. "Just one bite," she urged. "Please."

Against his better judgment, Silas took the plate. He stared at the potato for a long moment, his programming screaming at him to reject this foreign, inefficient object. But there was something in the woman's eyes, a spark of genuine, unadulterated hope, that made him hesitate.

Slowly, tentatively, he raised the potato to his lips and took a small bite.

And in that moment, something extraordinary happened. A piquancy, a real, honest-to-goodness flavor, exploded in his mouth. It was salty, it was savory, it was . . . delicious. His eyes widened in surprise, his carefully constructed world of flat obedience beginning to crumble around him.

He looked at the potato, then at the faces of the Foodies—their eyes fixed on him with a mixture of fear and hope. He saw not criminals, but people. People who had risked everything for a simple, human pleasure.

A slow smile spread across Silas's face. He took another bite of the potato, then another. The other Enforcers watched in stunned silence, their own programming in question.

The Enforcer next to Silas raised his rifle and laid down two quick, successive shots into the woman that wielded the potato. Turning to fix on Jean-Luc, the next shot froze the room in muted silence for what seemed an eternity. Smoke slowly wafted from the barrel of Silas's pistol, as his outstretched arm held the tool that secured the safety of the Foodies and their movement. One perfectly roasted potato had planted a seed. A seed of flavor, of joy, of humanity. And in a world that shunned non-conformity and variance, that was the most revolutionary thing of all.

63

SEEING IS BELIEVING

When I was nineteen, I was told I needed glasses and I was devastated. All my life I had been under the impression that only wimps, nerds, girls, and old people had to have corrected vision, so for me, this was tragic.

My mother took me to the optometrist, and after waiting forever, it was finally my turn to be humiliated. I couldn't see the letters on the chart. With either eye. Totally embarrassing!

Which is better? A or B? This one or this one? The first or the second?

Over and over until, finally, the doctor told me I was done. He'll call my mom when the glasses are ready.

A month later, we went back to the office to get the glasses and I begrudgingly put them on my face. It felt weird to have these plastic and glass things in front of me.

Touching me. Sitting on my nose. They were heavier than I had expected, and I didn't like them at all.

Sitting in the car as we drove home, I looked out at the landscape we passed by.

"Mom?"

"Yes, honey?"

"What are all those things on the trees?"

"Those are called leaves."

"Have they always been there?"

64

SELF-DEFENSE

"Do I need to remind you, Mr. Clinton, that you're under oath?"

"No, you do not. As crazy as this may seem, what I'm telling you is the truth."

"All right, then please tell the court one more time exactly what happened."

"I shot the sheriff, but I did not shoot the deputy."

"But three other witnesses say you did."

"No, like I already told you. I shot the sheriff, but I didn't shoot the deputy, I'm tellin' the truth, man."

"Then how do you account for what they're saying?"

"Everyone in town is trying to blame me. Tryin' to pin it on me. They all say I'm guilty of killing the deputy."

"And yet you deny it?"

"Yes."

"But you do admit to shooting the sheriff. Why did you shoot the sheriff?"

"Listen. I shot the sheriff, but I swear it was in self-defense. I had to protect myself. That sheriff hated me. Always had somethin' against me. An' I don't even know why."

"You expect us to believe that Sheriff Brown was trying to kill you and you acted in self-defense?"

"Yes, indeed. When he pulled me over, I might have been going a little over the speed limit, like maybe going fifty in a forty-five zone. I swear not a bit faster. All of a sudden I see that sheriff with his gun aimed at me. So, I shot him."

"You killed him?"

"It was self-defense. One hundred percent. Honest to God."

"Is that when the deputy arrived on the scene?

"Yes. I shot the sheriff, but not the deputy."

"Then who did?"

"Someone's lyin' 'cause I didn't do that. Look at the surveillance video. It shows clear as day what happened."

"I told you. The judge already ruled that the video will not be accepted as evidence."

"That makes no sense. There's a security camera that shows in broad daylight what happened. I have my rights."

"If you didn't shoot the deputy, then who did?"

"Had to be somebody else. After I shot the sheriff in self-defense, I put the gun down. It was after I put the gun down that the deputy was shot. It couldn't have been me. Quit messin' with me."

65

SELLING OUT

It wasn't intentional.

Ryan needed a job. Any job. He and his wife had just had a baby. There were bills to pay.

No jobs to be found in the sleepy little town of Jackson Hole.

Ryan and Willie grew up in the 1960's as ski bums hiking up the mountains with backpacks full of sandwiches, carrying their skis. It was rugged, wide-open wilderness. And they loved every minute of it. From the time they were fifteen and learned how to drive, even before they had an official drivers license, they would borrow Willie's dad's truck and drive as far up the trails as possible before hiking all morning to the top. Then spend all afternoon skiing back down to the truck. They were just young enough to miss the Vietnam draft, but old enough to be influenced by the cultural revolution they saw on TV going on across America. Sitting on top of the world they relished the freedom and dreamt of a future with endless opportunities. Would they become big time ranchers with thousands of cattle? Or would they head to the coast and make it big in the city? Anything was possible!

Then Ryan met Allison. They became inseparable and soon were engaged. Willie was best man at their wedding. Luckily he didn't tell any stories that were TOO embarrassing!

And then life happened as it does. Allison got pregnant. Without much of a prospect for jobs in a small mountain town, Ryan talked to Allison and soon they decided to move south to Denver. There was a much greater chance of finding a job in the growing city on the Front Range.

Willie helped them pack up their used Chevy.

"Well man, good luck! I hope you find a job quick! Gonna miss you bro."

"Thanks bud. Keep the dream alive!" Ryan replied.

Both friends secretly envied each other. Willie yearned to leave this small mountain town. Didn't matter where. Anywhere would be better than the middle of nowhere. But he had to look after his parents. His mom wasn't able to get around much anymore and his dad barely made enough money to pay for the house. Willie worked at the gas station and his paycheck went to the family to help out. Ryan never knew his happy go lucky friend was scraping by with his parents. He had his own troubles. Ryan wished so bad he could go back to the days of freedom. No responsibilities. The weight of being a husband and father weighed on his young shoulders.

66

SEVENTEENTH QUESTION

"Grandma, how did you meet Grandpa?"

"How did it happen?"

"Sit down over there, grab yourself a big glass of lemonade, and close your eyes. Tell me when you're ready."

"Okay, Grandma. I'm ready."

I'll never forget it. When I was sixteen, I went to the county fair without a care in the world. I was young, energetic, full of life and hope. I'm still not sure why, but I woke up that day expecting something grand, something fantastic, something life changing. But more than that, I woke up expecting someone.

I had enough money to get into the fair and buy a cola and a snack for lunch. But not enough to play any of the games or get a souvenir. Nothing like that. But for some reason, I had a hunch. A hunch that I would meet someone who would change my life. The strange part of my intuition was that it would be the seventeenth person who asked me a question. That's the person who would change the direction of my life.

The first question was at the entrance, "Do you want me to stamp your hand?" The second was a few minutes later, "Hey little lady, don't you want to try your luck at the ring toss?" And when I stopped for a drink of water, "Excuse me miss, can you tell me where the chicken exhibit is?"

I kept count of every question. Eight, nine, ten, eleven, and so on until sixteen. I just knew the next one would be magical. But nobody asked me any more questions. Not for a long time, and I began to doubt myself. I was sure there was going to be something special. I had dreamed of the number seventeen three nights in a row. And the third time convinced me. But something must have gone wrong.

I walked around the familiar places, visited the usual games and all the animal shows. When I went around the other side of the Ferris Wheel, there was a small boy sitting on a bale of hay crying. All by himself, nobody else around. Just sobbing. I kind of forgot all about my dream. I just wanted to help the little guy.

"Excuse me," I said. "Are you lost?"

He just looked at me.

"Is there something I can do to help?"

"Can you help me find my brother?"

"Well, I can try. Why don't you stand up and hold my hand, and we'll go look for him."

The little guy must have been only three or four years old, but he stood up and took me by the hand.

"Let's go get you some cotton candy, and we'll just walk around til you see your brother, okay?"

He nodded. And that's what we did. Just walked around, not talking at all, sharing the cotton candy because I just had enough money for one. Walked around for almost an hour. Then suddenly I heard some guy holler, "Hey Buddy! Over here! I've been looking for ya!"

The little boy yelled, "Jonathan!" and started running, right into the arms of a teenage boy who scooped him up and hugged him and kissed him, and I followed as fast as I could go. The little guy turned and pointed at me.

The older boy put Buddy down and came over to me. "I want to thank you for finding my brother and taking care of him."

"You're welcome," I smiled at him.

"I've been looking everywhere for the last hour or so and was ready to give up when I saw you through the crowd, and when you turned the corner, I saw Buddy holding your hand. I'd like to thank you for your kindness."

That's when it dawned on me. When the little boy asked if I could help find his brother, that was the seventeenth question I'd been asked at the fair.

"May I treat you to dinner and a few rides?"

Question eighteen.

"Umm, sure. I'd like that. But what about Buddy?"

"Oh, he'll be with us."

"Okay."

We spent as much time as we could together and six months later, on my seventeenth birthday, he asked me to marry him. Well, I had to get my pa's permission, but since Jonathan had a job by then, Pa said I could, and we've been married forty-two years now. I still can't figure it out, but for some unknown reason, I woke up knowing that question seventeen would change my life. I didn't know it would come from your Uncle Buddy. And I didn't know I would meet a boy who would later ask me to marry him, but it's been a grand, fantastic, and wonderful life.

"Wow, Grandma! I like that story."
"Me too, honey. Now give me a hug."

67

THE SHORTEST STORY ABOUT THE LONGEST TRIP

It's odd but I never would have guessed
this is what it feels like to sail around the world.

68

STUCK IN A MEMORY

Jordan opened his eyes and looked around. He slowly took in his surroundings, but nothing seemed familiar. Why was he sitting in this grassy field? The air was warm and thick, and the wild grass was tall but just short enough to see over it without standing up. He saw a couple of butterflies flittering around a few feet away. They appeared totally unbothered by his presence.

To his right, about fifty yards or so away, he saw a lone tree. It was leaning at roughly a 45-degree angle, and the leaves were beginning to change color. What kind of tree was it? Bah, he was never any good at remembering a single thing about trees. Trees were trees. What did it matter if it were an oak, a birch, a fir, or whatever?

Under the shade of the tree, he could just barely make out a signpost. While he didn't need glasses, the text on the sign was too small to make out from this distance. He wondered where he was.

The most disconcerting thing about waking up in a place without any memory is not that you don't know where you are. It's that, even with the confusion or memory loss, all the things you DO remember make you think that you ought to know where you are. There is a special kind of disquiet in knowing that you know yet don't know. Now he was confusing himself.

He didn't know where he was. He did know his name was Jordan. He knew the words for everything he saw before him. He didn't know where he was. Then an odd thought hit him. He didn't know WHEN he was. What year was it? He racked his brain, trying to remember anything other than names of things. History. Dates. The things that mark the existence of humanity in the universe.

He looked around again. He could label the grass, the butterflies, and the tree, but it felt…off. It felt know knowing ABOUT something yet not really KNOWING it. It was hard to conceptualize. He slowly ran his hand over the top of the wild grass, feeling the prickly sensation of the tips against the palm of his hand. The feeling seemed unlike anything he could pull from his fractured memory.

The wind blew gently, pushing the butterflies away from him. On the breeze he could smell the sweetness of the wildflowers that grew in the field. The scent was intoxicating. Why? He closed his eyes and tried to remember something – anything – that came before opening his eyes in that field.

"Jordan."

In his mind, he could hear a voice whisper his name.

"Jordan."

There was something familiar to the voice. Something sad.

"Jordan."

In a flash that exploded in his mind like the birth of a new star, he thought of a single word – "Grandpa!"

At that moment, something clicked in his brain and a flood of memories and thoughts came rushing in, intruders who barged in without knocking or asking permission. He realized why the grass and the tree felt familiar and strange at the same time. He knew them from school, but only from school. By the time he was born into the world, all flora and vegetation were strictly guarded in a government facility. Couldn't trust the general public with something so delicate. Humanity clearly showed it was incapable of maintaining such a fragile ecosystem as the planet. So, the world had become a habitat of metal, concrete, wires, and electronics. Only the government employees tasked with maintaining plant life would ever see, much less touch, something as precious as grass.

His thoughts returned to his grandfather. He suddenly remembered that his grandfather was on his deathbed, unable to speak because of the condition. He remembered the doctor's voice,

"Jordan, we have a procedure that will connect your mind to your grandfather's mind. Think of it like a closed-circuit communication device. We can hard-wire you to him. It should give you a chance to say goodbye before he passes."

His grandfather had been everything to Jordan. With the passing of his parents, his grandfather had been the one to raise him. In the chaos of the modern world, his grandfather had been his rock, filling his head with stories of the "old days," of trees, grasses, and butterflies – of the day he had proposed to Jordan's grandmother."

Jordan's eyes flew open. He KNEW this scene. His grandfather had told him this story over and over again since he was a boy. This wasn't real. This was a memory. But it wasn't even his memory – it was the memory of an old man lying in a hospital bed on the precipice of death.

Jordan screamed out loud. He stopped. Had he even really screamed? No. Because none of this was real. Well, in a sense it was real, but it wasn't REALLY real. He began to panic. He had no memory of the doctor telling him how to sever the connection to his grandfather. He suddenly started running as fast as he could towards the tree. Three feet beyond the tree, he smacked headfirst into a wall that was there but wasn't there. He stood up and slowly approached the spot. He could not move beyond it.

He smiled sadly to himself. This must be the edge of Grandpa's dream; the memory went no further. He looked around, unsure of what came next. The doctor never talked about this. At least, not that he could remember.

69

SUPERBOWL MVP

Even though they were favored to win, at half-time they were at the wrong end of a fourteen-to-nothing score, and the championship was on the line. Before the game, everybody in the world assumed the star running back would be Superbowl MVP, but he was having a bad game, fumbling three times in the first half. Another player on his team recovered one of the fumbles, but two of the dropped balls were picked up by the other team and returned for touchdowns. In addition to fumbling three times, he just seemed to be ineffective, like his mind was somewhere else.

In addition to a few defensive adjustments, the coach decided to make some changes on offense. They would focus more on passing than running and they would insert their second string running back. The starter had never been benched in his life. Humiliated, he slammed his helmet to the ground, pacing and cursing on the sidelines during the third and fourth quarters.

The new strategies paid off, though. On the opening drive of the second half, they moved down the field using mostly pass plays. The first time they ran the ball, the back-up ball carrier broke free for a twenty-three-yard touchdown. The defense held the opponent to three and out, and when they got the ball back, the sub ran for thirty yards, seventeen yards, and after a couple of passes, scored again, this time right up the middle for a twelve-yard score.

The fourth quarter was pretty much the same and by the time it was over, the favored team won the game twenty-eight to fourteen.

Their fans went crazy. The second-string running back was named the MVP of the game. Followers of the losing team were disheartened. Players on the winning team were shouting, dancing, pouring Gatorade on the coach, and partying in front of the TV cameras. Players on the losing team walked silently to the tunnel.

In the winners' locker room, the coach and players sprayed champagne, congratulated one another, took pictures, and gave interviews. Some cried, others laughed. Some phoned their friends, families, or lovers.

They all celebrated. One man did not.

70

THAT'S MY BOY

Jeez I can't believe this is really happening.
I'm too young for this! I'm not ready!
What am I going to do?!
Dang, how am I even supposed to tell which one is which?
Nurse! Nurse! Come over here please!
Behind the window . . . that one over there?
That's my boy?

Oh man it's cold.
Traffic was terrible!
I'm glad we made it with all this snow that just dumped on us!
Yes, yes, shhh. I'll be quiet.
Hey do you see him?
Up there on the left side . . . one of the Wise Men!
That's my boy!

Wha? Huh? Yeah I'll get it.
What time is it anyway?
Hello? They were doing what?!
Yes I'll be right over.
Hi. Oh don't worry I'll make sure it never happens again.
Yes officer. That one over there sitting on the bench.
That's my boy.

You got this buddy!
Shoot! Shoot! Shoot!
Stand up! For goodness' sake stand up!
Whew! That was close!
Hey man! Did you see that?
He's actually on the podium!
That's my boy!

Thank you all for coming today.
He always wanted to serve his country.
Man he sure looks sharp in his uniform.
Hadn't seen him since he shipped off.
His friends told me he never hesitated.
Three of them are alive today because of him.
That's my boy.

71

TOO MANY CONS

"I've heard it before, so don't give me any of that crap!"

"Whaddyamean?"

"Same old sob story. I'm innocent. But I'm not falling for it."

"But it's true."

"Yeah, yeah. That's what they all say."

"Whaddyamean?"

"Look. Call me jaded, insensitive, whatever you want, but I've listened to too many cons. I've heard too many lies. I've smelled too many rats. I'm no longer naïve. I know instinctively when someone isn't being honest. I just know."

"You just know, huh?"

As they walked the yard, a guard came up to the two of them.

"Which one of you is Johnson?"

"I am."

"We just got word you're getting out. Turns out you

really didn't commit the crime after all. Follow me."

"Yamean I'm goin' home?"

"Yup. Your boss is waiting for you in the visitors center."

"My boss?"

"Yup. The guy says he never doubted you and wants you to come back to work."

"You're kidding!"

"Your wife is here, too."

"Whaddyaknow! He was tellin' the truth!"

72

THE TRANSCRIPTIONIST

Have you ever noticed the people lingering at the periphery of major international business transactions or diplomatic conventions? Rows of booths line the walls, filled with a slurry of headphone-clad professionals. Those are translators, and they typically earn between $50,000 and $100,000 a year. Many are paid by the word. Some hold specialized qualifications—legal, medical, or fluency in multiple languages. But the most lucrative skills are often discretion—and a willingness to bend one's morals. Daniel White possessed all those skills and more.

By day, Daniel freelanced for top translation agencies, filling their most critical gaps and high-impact assignments. Whether the task involved complex multinational negotiations or obscure linguistic niches, Daniel was the unsung force keeping global transactions alive. He spoke thirteen languages fluently and could absorb the basics of a new one in as little as a week when needed. His grasp of legal, medical, architectural, and military terminology was so precise that many assumed he was an expert in each. Perhaps he was.

His day job was respectable enough—legitimate, steady, and dull. But Daniel's mind refused idleness. Without a complex system to unravel or a linguistic puzzle to devour, he grew restless. So at night, he sought sharper edges and higher stakes—as a transcriptionist.

Trusted for his discretion and quietly renowned among the world's most notorious organizations, his deft fingers and agile mind flew a mile a minute, turning raw audio into immaculate text in any typeface—or language—requested. It began two years earlier, when DMG Mori in Germany urgently needed translation support for a detailed contract involving cutting-machine tools and CNC-controlled lathes and milling systems. Daniel got the call.

Little did he know a prominent Yakuza emissary happened to be visiting the Japanese CEO—and witnessed Daniel in action. Daniel was professional, unflinching, and so precise in tone that he could imply threat or disdain with the slightest inflection. When the job was done, he bowed with cool formality, shook hands, and left. The Yakuza reached out discreetly soon after. Word spread quickly. Soon the Sinaloa Cartel, the Russian Bratva, and even the Hells Angels sought his services. Bound to no one, but usually accepting the offers, he only refused work with the Triads.

Transcriptionists listen to recorded audio and convert it into a text format. They use shorthand notes when listening to the recording, expand these for future use and edit their transcriptions prior to filing them.

Leaders across these organizations trusted Daniel with the most intimate details of their lives and operations. He captured every nuance, in any language, without flinching or betraying even a flicker of doubt—no matter how gruesome the content.

The true irony is that the US Intelligence and Law Enforcement Services enlisted Daniel's services, too. Terrorist threats, financial trails, decrypted banking chatter—whenever the FBI, CIA, NSA, or Homeland Security faced their toughest linguistic puzzles, they turned to Daniel. While it would be a conflict of interest for some, so divorced of emotion was he, spurred on by super-power-like OCD, that no one on the government side even had a hint that he was supporting the other side, too.

No one ever knew the real Daniel White—only his prodigious output from his nightly endeavors.

And that's how it remained until the day he died.

The unsung hero of international business and politics, the trusted guide through volatile multilingual negotiations, and the quiet key to dismantling some of the world's most dangerous criminals. So much of the interconnected world depended on Daniel. They never knew the breadth of his connections—and he never told.

73

THE TRAVELER

I remember that autumn day when the world burned down. Usually when I tell this story, people think I'm being hyperbolic. C'mon, man. Clearly the WORLD didn't burn down. This hunk of rock is still spinning in space. But when you're eleven years old and have never been anywhere other than the town in which you were born and raised, that town IS the world. And on that day, everything I knew went up in flames. Again, not being hyperbolic. I wish it were an exaggeration. I didn't know an entire town could go up in flames like that.

I don't suppose we could have seen it coming. I mean, no one did, so there's some comfort there. It's not like we saw the signs and ignored them. We were all caught off guard. Sure, like many catastrophes in life, this one was not spontaneous. Our world didn't end in a split second. Everything has an inception, and our cataclysm was no different. We just couldn't see it until after the fact. But everything seems clearer looking back. It's a lot harder to see clearly looking ahead. Looking back, I see now that it was all because of him.

Nobody knew his name. He just…appeared…one day, out of the nothingness on the edge of town. Yeah, I know, I know. There's more to the world past the edge of the town. I was eleven, remember? Cut me some slack. My family and I lived two blocks away from the town square, not far off the main street. Because my great-grandfather had helped build the first stores and houses in the town, we were considered one of the founding families. It didn't matter that the town had existed on paper before my ancestors arrived. As far as the living memory of the town was concerned, and that is all that really matters in small town USA, my family is near royalty. But I digress.

He just showed up. I guess if you had asked anyone who actually saw him arrive, they would have said that he stepped off the Number 2 bus at 4 p.m. The bus had a single stop in our town. But you'd be hard-pressed to find anyone who actually saw him arrive. Like I said, I wasn't being hyperbolic. I don't know how many people survived. Most of us lost everything; homes, pets, and family. I'm the last of my family, so any gaps you may find in my account are merely because I was freaking eleven and I've had to piece together what happened by talking to the couple dozen others who made it.

As I said, he just showed up. He didn't look all that different from everyone else passing through our town. No one came to our town to stay. You were born here. You died here. Anyone who was new was simply moving from one place to another. Indigents. Transitory people. That's all this guy was.

A traveler.

They say that when he stepped off the Number 2 that day, he had a smirk on his face. He stepped off, wearing that slightly crumpled light-grey suit with brown wingtip shoes. He had a fedora that fit the suit to perfection, the band around the hat an exact match to the shade of his shoes. His black-rimmed glasses perfectly fit his narrow face. There was nothing about him that was exceptional. Nobody gave him a second glance. He walked off the bus, carrying a brown satchel that also matched his fedora and shoes. Everything was coordinated to perfection.

In hindsight, that should have been a red flag to onlookers. Nobody in our town cared about that level of coordination. But in our town, there were no onlookers. Everyone was keen to mind their own business and stay out of the comings and goings of others, especially outsiders. Well, everyone except Mrs. Noland, the town gossip, but she lived on the other side of town from the bus stop and never saw The Traveler. Ironically, she was one of the few who survived.

The Traveler stepped off the Number 2 and walked across the street and stood in the shade of the oldest elm tree in town. He took out a handkerchief and wiped his brow which was damp from the heat of the Autumn afternoon.

Then he opened his satchel, and everything changed . . .

74

TWIST OF FATE

It had been four years and ten months since Marty and Kaylee had robbed the bank on the corner of Main Street. They had planned and planned, and then refined and refined the plan a few more times until they were a hundred percent certain it was foolproof. There's no way anybody, not even the keenest minds in law enforcement, would be able to figure out who did it.

"Seven hundred and forty-one thousand dollars!" Kaylee shouted again.

"I still can't believe it," Marty replied.

"How much interest will that bring in?" Kaylee wanted to make sure she understood the impact of their nest egg.

Marty had calculated thoroughly. "If we invest it at five percent, we get thirty-seven thousand dollars in interest the first year. And if we don't withdraw any of the money, it will compound so that the second year it makes thirty-nine thousand. The third year, it's forty-two thousand and it keeps getting bigger. After twenty years, the interest will be about ninety-eight thousand dollars per year, which is more than eight thousand per month."

"And that's when we retire, right?" Kaylee was forty-eight years old and liked the idea of retiring before she was seventy.

"That's right." Marty was a year younger, and just as eager to kiss his working days goodbye.

The money was at a self-storage in Kerrington, Kansas while they waited for the statute of limitations to kick in. Only two more months and then it's all theirs. But Marty was getting antsy.

"What can go wrong?" he wondered aloud.

"Absolutely nothing." Kaylee was sure. "We've gone over this a zillion times. We covered everything, right?"

"Yeah. I know, but . . ."

"But what, Marty? You're not freaking out, are you?"

"I'm just getting nervous is all."

"Well, relax. We did everything right. The money is in fireproof, waterproof ammo boxes. The federal and state statute of limitations is five years, so in two months, there's nothing anyone can do to us. We drive up to Kerrington, get our money, and then start investing. What's there to worry about, hmmm?"

"You're right. Okay, I'll settle down."

But down inside . . . he still worried.

They waited a month after the five-year anniversary of the crime, just to make sure. They stopped for the night in a small hotel in Guthrie, OK. The next day, as they drove north towards Kerrington on Interstate 35, the music on the radio was interrupted by a news bulletin about another potential tornado sweeping through Kansas, but it didn't seem to be where they were going. Kaylee's excitement increased as Marty's apprehension worsened. When they arrived at the self-storage, they saw that the roof of the building had been ripped off. They went to their unit and found all of their ammo boxes unmolested, so they loaded them into the back of Marty's SUV.

As they pulled onto the road, suddenly two police cars pulled up behind them and two others came from in front of them. Marty stopped at the side of the road and four officers surrounded the car, all four with guns pointed at Marty and Kaylee.

"Get out of the car! Now!" one of the cops shouted.

"What's going on?" Marty demanded.

"A tornado came through here a couple of weeks ago. The insurance company came to inspect everything and secure the stuff stored here, and they noticed your ammo boxes, so they called us to take a look. We installed cameras and have been watching the place to see if anyone shows up. Seems like you're the people who robbed the First Waco Federal Bank five years ago."

"Officer, even if we did that, that was more than five years ago. Isn't there a statute of limitations?"

"You're right. But the statute doesn't apply if someone dies during the crime."

"What are you talking about?" Kaylee interjected.

"Ma'am, you might not know it, but during the robbery the bank manager had a heart attack and died as the thieves made their getaway. That means there is no time limit regarding when you can be prosecuted for the crime. Ironically, had you come a few weeks ago, before the tornado, we would never have known the loot was stashed here, and you'd have gotten away with it. But now, you're both under arrest."

75

VORTEX OF NEGATIVITY

When the staff met on Friday afternoons, they always ended up arguing and fighting. Name calling, criticizing, swearing, insulting. You name it. They were the epitome of a dysfunctional work group and everybody knew it. But nobody knew what to do or cared enough to do anything about it.

Mark had worked there about three years. At first, it bothered him and he tried to help steer the bickering in a more productive direction, but it's almost impossible to effect lasting change when the official leadership of the organization intentionally keeps things ugly and hurtful.

He had thought many times about leaving, just finding work elsewhere, but each time felt that would not be the best course of action. So when the meetings tended to get heated, he zoned out and did his best to ignore it, to varying degrees of success, of course. Some days he got sucked into the vortex of negativity and participated 100%.

Today, however, no matter what they did or said, regardless of what they literally threw at each other, he sat there with a grin and a faraway look in his eye as if he was daydreaming about being in Hawaii or some tropical island basking in the sun without a care in the world. And his demeanor bothered them.

"Mark! Wake up! Are you with us? Hello? What's the matter with you? Say something!"

Mark looked at them with that silly grin on his face and said nothing. Finally, the big boss couldn't take it anymore. He shouted in Mark's direction.

"Mark! What's wrong with you? Doesn't any of this matter?"

"No, sir. It does not. In fact, nothing you all are talking about, screaming about, bashing each other about matters at all."

"Is that so! And why are you so smug, self-righteous, and above it all?"

"Well, sir, it's like this. About a month ago, I was right here with you all, behaving exactly like every one of you are today. You know that. I've been here three years and fit right in, right? But I started feeling like I needed something more in my life. So I prayed and asked God if he was real to show me something, somehow. And he did. That night I had a dream about what it meant to have real peace inside. The next Sunday I went to a church near my house and I felt something stirring inside of me and I started to feel different. Like that peace in my dream was starting to be real in my mind and throughout my life. I told my girlfriend and she said she could see the change in me and wanted to experience it too, so she went to church with me. Last night she asked me to marry her and I said yes. So what we tend to argue about during these Friday staff meetings? Well, it really doesn't matter anymore. It's foolish and meaningless and doesn't accomplish anything. Look, I didn't come here to preach to you. In fact, as you could see, I tried real hard to say nothing. But since you practically ordered me to explain myself, boss, I decided to let you know. I don't condemn or judge any of you. But I really do feel like I have grown bigger than the pettiness we display in here week after week. Since I have to be here per your orders, sir, I will participate when we're actually talking about work, but when we devolve into immature, interpersonal, nasty stuff, well, I don't have to do any of that. I've come to love and care about everyone here and will be a friend, not anything else."

Everyone sat there in stunned silence. The boss sat there tapping on the conference room table trying to take in all that Mark had said. Then he spoke.

"What you said makes sense. I've noticed a change in you, too. In fact, if you're willing to make a commitment to stay a year, I'd like you to become my assistant and head up these weekly staff meetings. What do you think?

"Well, sir. This comes as a total surprise, but if you're willing to let me set the tone and make a few changes to how we do things, I just might be willing."

76

A WARM AFTERNOON

As is usually the case, as soon as the "Fasten Seat Belt" lights go dark, the rush begins: unclick seat belts, get out of chairs, open overhead bins, pull down overstuffed carry-ons without whomping anyone on the head. Then comes the long wait for the plane to pull up to the gate and the doors to open, followed by the exodus.

This time, however, one person stayed on board. She never pulled down her overstuffed carry-on, never opened the overhead bin, never got out of her chair, and never unclicked her seat belt. Somewhere over the Atlantic, she had gone into a coma and nobody noticed. The coma lasted twelve years.

One warm afternoon at the Assisted Care facility where she was "living" her eyes opened and she screamed. "Help! Call the police! Someone help me!"

Attendants and nurses came running. They all knew Rita. They all had taken turns with her daily sponge bath.

They all were there the day the OB/GYN did the C-section and her baby girl was born. They all wondered whether her friends and family even cared after all this time. And they had all given up expecting her to ever return to consciousness.

The resident physician asked her, "Why should we call the police?"

"Because Billy's trying to kill me!"

"Who is Billy?"

"My husband. We've been married two weeks and are on our way home from the honeymoon."

"How did he try to kill you?"

"He injected me with something; I don't know what it was. I felt the sting and looked down to see a syringe in my arm. Then he put a pillow over my face to suffocate me. A few seconds later, everything got fuzzy mentally, I started hallucinating, and I fell asleep. I'm just now waking up. Where am I?"

"We're in your hometown, Rocky Mount, North Carolina, at an Assisted Care facility."

"What? How long have I been here?"

"Twelve years."

"Twelve years? Where's Billy?"

"Rita, we've never met Billy."

"Hand me my purse, please."

"When you came here, you didn't have a purse. All you had were the clothes you were wearing when the plane landed. Your parents come to visit every Monday."

"What day is it?"

"It's Monday. They should be here in ten minutes."

77

WHAT LOVE LOOKS LIKE

AHHHHH

FLEEEEAAAAASSSSS!

The call came late.

Rob was packing his bags for the trip to New York.

Andrea was at her house across town.

They were supposed to be heading to upstate New York for Rob's little brother's wedding first thing in the morning. Andrea didn't even really want to go but she knew it was important to Rob. She hated big crowds and having to be "on" for social settings. Nobody ever knew it because she was so kind and engaging. But Rob knew. And he didn't take it for granted.

So when the call came at 9:45 PM his first reaction was, "maybe you should cancel the trip. I can go and I'll meet you after the wedding and we'll take care of it."

"No. I still can go. I know it's important. My whole day just fell apart! I was so happy today. It was such a relaxing day! Then before I finished packing I figured I'd give Arnold a bath."

Arnold was a 15 year old yellow lab who had been Andrea's dog since he was a puppy. He was family. He was old and only ate soft food. But he was still a happy dog and the goodest boy ever.

"So I went to give Arnie a bath and fleas started jumping off him like he was a sinking ship"

"Eww gross!"

"yeah no kidding. It was baaaaaddd! I am holding him under the water with one hand, practically drowning the poor old guy. With my other hand I was trying to order flea shampoo and medicine but it's too hard to do that and try to wash him. Will you order me some stuff?"

"I think if I try to order it, it will be too late and the store will close. I'm getting my shoes on. I'm on the way now."

78

WHAT'S MY QUESTION

| . . . | . . . | . . .

The blinking line "insertion point" in his Word document seemed to taunt him.

"What is your question? What are you going to type? You don't know, do you? You don't have any f*!@#$% idea."

It would be maddening if it weren't accurate in its torment; instead, it was simply demoralizing… depressing.

Enrique was a straight-A student throughout high school and finished his bachelor's with a 3.98 GPA. His master's work was more tailored to literature than education, but he was breezing through it and already had his sights higher.

The Gonzalez family was bright, and after seven generations in Chesco, just south of Philly, it was hardly accurate to call them immigrants anymore. Still, the brown skin and trace of an accent never stopped others from exuding prejudice onto them.

Enrique's great-great-grandfather had been the first in his family to attend college. His great-grandfather earned an MD and served at the Children's Hospital of Philadelphia. Two of his aunts became attorneys, and his father had always encouraged him to pursue an MBA and join him in business. Instead, Enrique pursued an MA Lit/MSEd combo wondered whether he might teach someday. Maybe at a university? Maybe after he proved himself—did something that made him feel qualified and acceptable.

It was the "maybe" part that trapped him.

"I know I love academia. I love learning. I love sharing that love to help others learn. And higher ed is practically in my blood. If I spend a few more years of school, I'll be better qualified for professor positions, I'll get to learn more, and maybe I'll figure out what I really want."

Talking himself into the resolve to pursue a PhD was the easy part. Now he had to choose a specific question—one worth answering—and build a research proposal around it. Choosing and deciding from among options had never been a strong suit. Enrique even avoided Starbucks because their menu overwhelmed him, preferring instead the simple certainty of a Nespresso variety pack at home.

It was now September, and he would finish his master's program in the spring. PhD applications—proposals included—were due in a couple of months. It was already September.

Every few days, after mustering the motivation to open the blank document, the blinking cursor stabbed at his thoughts like a large-gauge needle through the eye. At least he'd named the document, so he could reopen whenever he worked up the courage. Its title: "Draft Research Proposal – Enrique Gonzalez."

He still had nothing.

| . . . | . . . | . . .

"What's my question?"

He leaned back, rubbing his eyes, letting the silence settle. All his life, he'd waited to feel qualified before stepping forward. But maybe the question wasn't something he found. Maybe it was something he grew into.

He placed his hands on the keyboard. The cursor blinked. He blinked back.

"Fine," he whispered. "Let's figure this out together."

And for the first time, the blank page felt less like a threat and more like an invitation.

79

WHERE AM I

His job sent him to interior Alaska for a month-long assignment. North of Denali, and away from the insulating effects of the coast, the days averaged thirty below, with a few nights dipping into the -50s with wind chill. The days were brutally cold, the winter sun shone only briefly, and the workdays were long—starting and ending in darkness.

Everything about the work was difficult, and as fatigue set in, it became easy to lose sight of the precautions meant to guard against the cold. Out of the 7,000+ workforce, over 200 of them sustained some form or fashion of a cold weather injury. Most cases were contact frostbite—below -20, a single touch of a metal surface causes instant cell death. There were a few cases of hypothermia, a few of immersion foot, plenty of chilblains, and everyone felt the chill settle into their bones at some point.

By the end of the month, everyone was spent and more than ready to go home. His flight out was scheduled for 1 a.m. on Delta. With such a late departure, it wasn't worth trying to sleep before-hand, so he simply went out with the team for a few drinks after dinner and bide the time before heading to the airport.

By the time he checked in, along with seventeen others from his team, they were walking zombies, barely aware enough to check bags, clear security, and find the gate. Once in their seats, they all dozed off.

Falling asleep on a plane is seldom easy, especially after turning thirty. After forty, it was practically impossible. But the long month and the late night, early morning departure was a different beast entirely. He was out cold before takeoff for the four-hour flight.

A voice on the loud speaker registered, but the words were all muffled and non-sensical. The attendant roused him, and the voice overhead began to sharpen. Everyone was getting off the plane.

"Please make sure to secure your carry-ons, personal item, and all of your belongings. More information will be provided at the gate regarding later flights."

Some of his teammates were still asleep, but the attendant was already moving toward them. Everyone else was shuffling toward the front of the plane.

When he stepped off the passenger boarding ramp, he looked around. He'd been through the Seattle-Tacoma airport more times than he cared to remember, but nothing about this place looked familiar. Confused and still tired, he tried to make sense of what he was seeing.

"Where am I?"

He stumbled forward to make room for the others debarking behind him, squinting and trying to make out something familiar. Finally, he saw some familiar faces. Others from work, not teammates from his flight, were standing near the adjacent gate. Though still hazy, he could now make out the voice on the loud speaker.

The crew was unable to de-ice the plane, and after over two hours sitting in the cabin, they determined it was unlikely they could complete the flight before the pilots' crew-rest window expired.

Ground crews would continue trying to thaw the plane, and once the flight crew received the minimum required rest, the aircraft would be rescheduled for that afternoon. Any chance of making their connecting flight in Seattle was out the door, and their ultimate destination only had one flight a day.

He already had only two days to see his family before the next work trip. Now with the delay, he'd have a single day to do laundry, stow the arctic gear, pack for a stint in the tropics, and somehow see his family somewhere in between.

He couldn't stifle the groan.

And they'd already turned in the rental vehicles. Now there were logistics to untangle just to find somewhere to lie down for a few hours before returning to the airport to try again later.

He rubbed his eyes, trying to blink the world into focus. The terminal lights felt too bright, the carpet too loud, the air too thin. He checked the time, then checked it again, as if the numbers might rearrange themselves into something merciful.

They didn't.

He exhaled, long and slow. One day at home. One day to reset an entire life before the next trip. It wasn't enough. It never was. But it was something.

He hitched his bag higher on his shoulder and let out a humorless laugh. "At least the tropics won't need de-icing," he muttered.

The thought wasn't comforting, exactly, but it nudged him forward. One step, then another. First order of business: find coffee strong enough to resurrect the dead. Then figure out where he could crash for a few hours. Then—somehow—make the most of the single day waiting for him on the other end of all this.

He wasn't sure how he'd pull it off. But he was moving again, and for now, that was enough.

80

WHITE MONSTERS

"CcccRICK fsssshhhhh"

When the weather was warm, nothing quenched his thirst quite like an icy cold white Monster Ultra.

"CcccRICK fsssshhhhh"

When working in Alaska throughout the frozen month of February, there was a simple pleasure of opening up a can of his favorite energy drink. Most enjoyable cold, if he forgot to chill it before going to work for the day, he'd leave it on top of the car while plugging in the engine warmer, raising all the wiper blades, and grabbing his gear. The few minutes of tasks in the sub-zero temperatures were enough to bring the drink's temperature down to an appropriate level.

"CcccRICK fsssshhhhh"

The sound of a pleasant pick-me-up and his morning routine. Hot coffee was great and had its own place—usually first thing in the morning. After the coffee were a few cups of water, and by mid-morning, it was time for the Monster.

"CcccRICK fsssshhhhh"

81

WHITEOUT

Squeezing the steering wheel like he was wringing a chicken's neck, Brayden's knuckles were solid white (not that he had ever actually strangled a chicken). A combination of a vise-like death grip and the already delayed capillary-refill due to the arctic conditions inside and outside his Subaru Outback. Waves of white blew across the road as the wind continually picked up more of the freshly fallen powder off the top of the snow-drenched countryside around him.

"Can you please swing by the niuvirvik [by which she meant NorthMart] on your way home? There's supposed to be a storm rolling in, and we're starting to run low on milk, diapers, produce, and rice. We're good on meat, flour, frozen veggies, and just about everything else." Kimalu's tone was nothing out of the ordinary.

An innocuous request that normally wouldn't mean much. Whether he got it on his way home, or simply went back out to the-place-to-buy-things (A.K.A. "niuvirvik"), he could pick those things up whenever.

Brayden was born and raised in Anchorage, so you'd think he'd be as weather savvy as they come. But he married a Canadien girl from Eureka the week before graduating at the University of Alaska (Anchorage) and followed her homeward after graduating last year. He quickly realized that living at -20 was different than living in the +10 to +65 he was used to. During his first year in Nunavut, he had lucked out and never experienced a flash-onset storm.

Their love wasn't really the stuff of romcoms, except that he was fond of her and pursued her for three years before she even really noticed. As far as Nunavut girls go, they're on the level and not prone toward wanton shows of emotion. That's one of the things he liked about Kimalu, but it made for an undramatic and rather even-keeled courtship. A lot of transactional conversations and interactions accounting for their needs and general preferences. But nothing effusive or "love is in the air" kind of romance.

It took all of four months after getting married before Kimalu became pregnant, and nine months later, there was their perfectly formed, ten-fingered, ten-toed daughter Nuka. Nuka was a unisex Inuit name meaning "firstborn," but Brayden liked the sound of it, even aside from its functional accuracy describing his firstborn child. Brayden could recall clear as day Kimalu telling him she was pregnant, and the spectrum of emotions that he processed—mostly individually—over the next few months.

"Brayden . . ."

"Yes Kimalu?"

"We're pregnant."

No effusive emotion... no scenario or buildup. Just a nonchalant evening announcement after getting ready for bed and coming out of the bathroom. It was so crystal clear because he'd always heard stories about fanciful or elaborate "reveals." Though not prone to emotionality, he kind of liked the idea. Nevertheless, that was not his reality.

At first, he was in disbelief or at least emotionally non-responsive; rather, he accepted the fact.

A week later, he was curious and couldn't help but research the entire gamut of being a new parent, to include: babies, newborns, breast feeding, how to change a diaper, how to get babies to go to sleep, how to keep the romance alive among new parents, how to put a cup on a baby boy so urine doesn't rain all over you, and all manner of other pro tips he never otherwise would have thought to learn.

A month later he was apprehensive and sure he would get it all wrong. There were a lot of calls to Mom and Dad that month as they reassured him and he came to grips with the fact that he would do everything wrong, but that it's OK. Man... parenting is hard. And he didn't even have a kid yet.

Right around the end of the first trimester, he started to regain his composure and emotional bearing. Which was also right around the time that Kimalu started getting all kinds of hormonal and as a side effect, emotionally unstable.

So much of the recent past was running through Brayden's head as he looked into a wall of white and let off the gas.

"Lord, please help me get through this storm alive and get back to Kimalu and Nuka."

The prayer was short, sweet, and sincere, and he meant it from the bottom of his heart. There was nothing Brayden could do to control the weather, and he realized full well that had he simply gone to NorthMart from work before getting home, instead of realizing as he pulled into the driveway that he had no milk, diapers, or produce in the car, he probably would be warm and safe inside his house with his calm, loving wife, and his sweet, innocent, usually even-tempered baby.

Instead, here he was inching forward while the inches accumulated on the road and countryside before him. A mere three more miles to go, but failing to get home, whether veering off, getting stuck on the shoulder, or colliding with an unlikely but possible oncoming car . . . any one of those would mean certain death on a night like this.

To whatever extent Brayden could see in front of him, whether it was five or fifty feet, the effect was the same. It was pure white as far as the eye could see.

He didn't even think it was blowing all that hard anymore, but the snowfall made an even blanket across the road that made it impossible to tell the shoulder from the ditch or the tundra around him. About the only thing he could make out were occasional trees.

His grip tightened more before he made a deliberate decision to relax so he didn't cause an accident that might not otherwise happen.

The storm knocked out local cell service, too.

Brayden's phone never rang, and Kimalu's message didn't get to him while before he lost service.

"Whether you're at work or at the niuvirvik, just stay put. We're fine on things for the next day or two, but you really shouldn't be driving tonight. Just wait where you are, and come back after they clear the roads in the morning. We love you and look forward to seeing you soon. Stay safe."

82

THE WIDOW

"Can I please just have oooooone more?" Harper pleaded.

Looking out the apartment window as the rain clouds smothered what light remained in the already gray city, Alyssa replied, her annoyance unmistakable, "You said that last time . . . And the time before."

"Pleeeeeeeeeese? I won't ask for anything else ever again."

The number of times the little girl had broken that promise matched the number of times she'd made it. Still, Alyssa caved, squeezing her eyes tightly shut and wishing away the migraine that no amount of coffee or cigarettes could cure.

A familiar refrain echoed in her mind—Jackson never would have been so soft or feeble as to give in to a four-year-old. Why did it have to be like this?

83

WORDS OF HOPE

Nobody believed in Ricardo. From the time he was four, he felt disrespected. Nobody expected him to succeed. He wanted to run away or end his life.

But instead of quitting, he studied, disciplined himself, and returned scorn with graciousness. Occasionally, someone would encourage him, and he would write it down. When his notebook contained a hundred messages of motivation, encouragement, or inspiration, he wrote a book titled One Hundred Words of Hope. It became a bestseller and sold 2.3 million copies, leading to interviews and talk show appearances.

Everyone called him an overnight success. But he knew the truth.

84

WORLD'S BEST BURGER

"Did you see the ad on your Facebook feed?"

"That's like asking if I saw the tall guy on the basketball team. Which ad are you talking about?"

"The one about the hamburger contest."

"What? No, I didn't. What did it say?"

"Here, take a look."

"They're having a contest?"

"Yeah."

"For a new hamburger?"

"They want to offer a brand-new item to their menu, and they're going to pay a million dollars to whoever sends in the best recipe. AND there's another million for whoever names the new hamburger."

"Is this for real?"

"Yeah, and I figured with your experience for making the best burgers any of our friends have ever tasted, you might want to enter the contest."

"And you?"

"Well, I'll come up with the name."

"I love it."

"But there's something else."

"What?"

"We've been dating for, like, more than a year now, right?"

"Yeah."

"So, I think maybe we make a deal."

"A deal?"

Yeah, if either one of us wins a million bucks, how 'bout we get married?"

"Wow! I was NOT expecting that."

"How 'bout it?"

"Are you for real?"

"Yeah, you know I love you."

"Well, then. I have a counter proposal."

"Okay . . ."

"Let's do the contest, but why don't we plan on getting married regardless of the outcome?"

"Really?"

"I love you too. We've been saying the only thing holding us back from getting married is the money, but shoot, maybe it's time we realize love is more than money and just make it official?"

"YES!"

He entered the contest online, submitted his recipe, and waited. And waited.

They got married at the church on the corner, about twenty-eight friends in attendance. Poor, but very happy.

One night as he was grilling burgers, the phone rang. His recipe won the contest. They danced and cried and shouted and made love and drank iced tea because they couldn't afford champagne or even cheap wine.

There would be a news conference the following week to announce it to the world and kick off the second part of the contest.

"Well, Babe? What are you going to call it?"

85

WORTH A DAMN

Devon had a sudden realization that he was flat on his back, lying in the dirt. He opened his eyes. At least – he thought he opened them. Oh, yeah, there it was. He opened them. The world was blurry but was slowly coming into focus. He sat up and, as his vision continued to clear, he looked around. He had no idea where he was or even how he had come to be here – wherever here was.

The air was hot and thick, almost like you could cut it with a dull knife. The sun was high in the sky. There were no buildings around as far as his now-adjusted eyes could see. In fact, there was absolutely nothing around. He was on a dirt road in the middle of a barren field of dirt. Dirt on top of dirt. He found himself sitting at the intersection of two dirt roads.

He suddenly popped up in excitement and understanding. This was just an intersection. It was THE CROSSROADS! His memory, though moving more slowly than his vision, was now beginning to clear. He had just been lamenting how everyone else in his life had been catching breaks, but nothing ever went his way. He had even hired a life coach to help him get on track. That was the last thing Devon remembered. He had been sitting in his life coach's office for his bi-weekly session.

"Devon, what EXACTLY is it that you're hoping to do with your life?"

"Look, I know it's not sexy, but I want my work to really take off, to be noticed by people that matter. Sitting in my cubicle until I retire or die, serving some conglomerate I never see or understand is not what I want in life. I want to influence the world!"

"Those are lofty goals. I guess the real question is, 'How far are you willing to go to achieve them?"

Sitting on a faded, overstuffed loveseat that reflected Devon's life, out of place and not really belonging, Devon threw his hands up in the air. "Well, I've got nothing else going for me so I might as well go all. I'd sell my soul for making it to the big leagues of graphic design."

With an impish smile, the life coach raised his hand and snapped his fingers. Now Devon was at THE CROSSROADS.

In the distance, walking through the hazy heat, a lone figure was moving his way. Devon's heart started racing. He knew this story. He knew that the Devil met at THE CROSSROADS to buy your soul and give you your heart's desire. He had always thought the story was nonsense. But it was real now, wasn't it? I mean, lots of myths and fairy tales are grounded in a kernel of truth and reality, right?

Sooner than humanly possible, the lone figure was standing right in front of Devon. At the sight of him, Devon's heart sank. He saw that the figure was a little man, about five feet tall. He was balding and wore what was left of his hair in a stringy combover. He was wearing a wrinkled light gray suit with a fire-engine red tie that looked worn and faded. The only parts of the man's appearance that was sharp were his shoes. His black patent leather shoes were shined to a mirror finish, even in this dry and dusty landscape.

The man saw Devon eyeing his shoes.

"Ah, well, you know what they say. Shoes make the man!" The man chuckled softly at his own joke.

"Are you one?" Devon asked.

"Am I one what?" the man seemed a little impatient. Devon found it a little off putting. After all, he WAS here to sell his soul. The least this little man could do was show some patience.

"Are you…a man? I thought I was supposed to meet the Devil at THE CROSSROADS."

The little man cleared his throat. "Ah, well, business has been BOOMING lately, and the boss can't possibly do all the work by himself. I am what you might call a lesser demon. I handle the bulk of the paperwork, implement corporate strategy, and facilitate growth and change to enhance to big picture. It's all about synergy."

"I'M SELLING MY SOUL TO MIDDLE MANAGEMENT?!?!" Devon was livid. He wasn't actually sure what he was expecting, but it surely wasn't this. He had thought selling one's soul was more…dignified? Maybe that wasn't the right word, but this was NOT it.

The little man cleared his throat again. "Well, my young friend, shall we begin? You want to influence the world, yes? Let's talk terms and agreement!"

Devon sighed. He already felt like his corporate job had sucked the life out of him, so what difference did it make to sell his actual soul? "Fine. Let's proceed."

The little man hummed to himself as he manifested a briefcase and pulled out a manila folder. It was labeled D. Wilson. "Now, Dylon, I've been taking a look at your file, and it seems like we can offer you an OUTSTANDING compensation package with some fringe benefits to boot. I really think you'll be tickled with what we're proposing."

Devon paused. "Devon."

"What?"

"Devon. My name is Devon. You just called me Dylon. I'm Devon Wilson."

The little man scowled deeply. "Oh, no. No no no no no no no. This is terrible. This is just awful. Looks like someone made a clerical error. Had to have been Gladys. She's always messing up my paperwork! I'd kill her if, well, you know." He smiled at Devon apologetically. He dug into his briefcase and pulled out another folder. "Ah, here we are. DEVON WILSON."

Devon had a moment of clarity and saw that, no matter where he was, all middle management was the same. He had thought his life was hell. Now, here at THE CROSSROADS, he was beginning to think that it was all hell. He realized the little man was snapping his fingers to get Devon's attention.

"Well, Mr. Wilson, after looking at your correct record, I'm afraid that we have nothing to offer you at this time. Please wait the allotted six months and then you're welcome to renegotiate."

Now Devon was furious. "What do you mean nothing to offer?!? I'm selling my soul!"

The little man cleared his throat again. "Well, the thing is, you've not lived a great life. You aren't a stellar person, you regularly mistreat others, and there's not one redeeming thing about you. Truth be told, it looks like you were headed our way regardless, so there's no benefit for the boss to try to snag your soul himself. You're putting in all the work! It's just not cost-beneficial for us to make this deal. What I'm trying to say, Mr. Wilson, is that your soul just isn't worth a damn."

86

CLOSE THE DOOR ON YOUR WAY OUT

Though he would never admit it, opera spoke to Eric and touched his soul in a way words could never express. He wasn't embarrassed about it, but as a matter of self-preservation, he kept his inner drama enthusiast under wraps.

"I guess I'm a closet thespian," Eric mused, tickled with his own droll humor. He was straight, no doubt about it, but loved a good play on words. And he loved to sing.

Eric lived two hours northeast of Atlanta in Stephens County, and just last year, the principal disbanded the school's performing arts clubs and cancelled the drama department. The local sets of 59 Brim Bloods and Rollin 60s Crips, though hell-bent on killing each other, regularly jumped in new recruits by targeting performers. The more flamboyant or theatrical the student, the bigger the target. A few years earlier, one of Eric's older brother's classmates had been killed in just such an initiation. Those gangs were the worst part of living in Toccoa and made life there almost unbearable.

Just one more year to go, and he could graduate and get out of there, finally free to be himself. His bold, boisterous, bass-baritone self. He just couldn't at this juncture in time.

His grades were good. Not great, but solid. And he did just enough math and science to get by. But he loaded up on music and languages, working ahead until he'd taken all the French and Italian the school offered, eventually requesting special permission to study German remotely through a school on the other side of Atlanta. After finishing the assigned homework, most nights he'd pick his way through Bizet and Berlioz, Verdi, Wagner, and Wolfgang Amadeus Mozart. The French and Italian operas were breezy reading, their scores leaping off the pages and straight into his heart. German was still difficult, but knowing much of the music already made the words easier to tackle.

Early in the spring, as basketball season wound down, there was a gang-related shooting in the parking lot after one of the games. Eric didn't know the victims, but the incident reminded him to keep his passion on the down-low and sharpened his urgency to finalize his escape plan. UGA's Hugh Hodgson School of Music offered a performance-based scholarship he was determined to earn. It was only a matter of practice.

He began staying after his eighth-period music class to work on his audition. Weeks away from graduation, while practicing in his happy place, the door opened and two thugs walked in.

"Yo. Who you, and wha' dya doin'?"

Eric froze.

He'd been so excited to practice that he didn't notice his classmates hadn't closed the door all the way, and his music was spilling out into the hall.

Before him were five arias meant to showcase his bass-baritone fach. But nothing from Gounod, Rossini, or Mozart in front of him was going to get him out of this predicament. And nothing about his taste in music would ease the tension of this moment.

Orff's "O Fortuna" was on blast in the internal soundtrack of his mind.

Sors immanis
Et inanis
Rota tu volubilis
Status malus
Vana salus
Semper dissolubilis

But it wasn't just in his mind. Eric was so stressed, he was belting out the Latin lyrics with more passion, volume, and intensity than any of the pieces he had been practicing only moments earlier.

"Dude! Dude! That's that song from the movies! Like . . . 6 Underground. I just watched it two nights ago." The first thug smacked his friend's shoulder, excited by the music and recognizing it from a movie he'd seen on Netflix less than forty-eight hours ago.

Eric's heart pounded so hard, he could hear his own pulse. The muffled sound of the two muttering as they walked out was cut short when the door finally clicked shut, sealing off all sound.

Music nearly got him killed that day—but it also saved his life. When the door finally clicked shut behind the two boys, Eric stood there trembling, breath shallow, heart still pounding in his ears like timpani. The room felt smaller, the air thinner, as if the danger had squeezed the space around him.

But then he looked at the door. Closed. Sealed. Silent.

A door left open had almost ended everything. A door closing had given him another chance.

He let out a shaky laugh. Music had betrayed him, exposed him, nearly delivered him straight into the hands of people who would never understand him. But music had also been the only language powerful enough to disarm them. It was ridiculous. It was terrifying. It was perfect.

He gathered his sheet music with steadier hands. One day, he promised himself, he'd walk through a different door—one he chose, one that opened into a world where his voice wasn't a liability but a gift.

For now, he locked the practice room behind him.

And for the first time, he understood that the right doors don't just open. Sometimes they close to show you where you're meant to go next.

ABOUT THE AUTHORS

Jeff William Linzey is a Brazilian Jiu Jitsu Black Belt, board-game strategist, and award-winning guacamole craftsman who was once voted by his law school class as "the one I'd least want to oppose at trial." Aside from his JD, his ties to learned professions further extends to being a licensed minister, and beyond a tendency to research and self-diagnose ailments, he married an ER nurse. His professional writing has been recognized as one of the ten best of its semicentennial and republished in the 50th Anniversary Edition, but this collection marks his first published work of fiction—unless you count the children's story he co-wrote with his four imaginative kids. Jeff lives with his wonderful wife, their four fantastic children, and an ever-growing stack of books he swears he'll finish soon.

Christopher J. Linzey is a Navy chaplain, author, speaker, and lifelong student of the stories people carry. With more than a decade of military chaplaincy experience across the Army Reserve, Navy, and Marine Corps, he has served Sailors, Marines, and families through deployments, training commands, counseling sessions, ceremonies, and the everyday moments that shape life. His ministry and writing are driven by a conviction that meaning is often found in ordinary people facing extraordinary circumstances, and that humor, hope, struggle, and grace often show up together. Christopher previously co-authored *Getting It Twisted*, a collection of short stories, and co-authored *Military Ministry*, a practical textbook designed to equip and train the next generation of military chaplains.

When he is not writing, Christopher spends his time speaking, creating digital content, mentoring leaders, playing music, and asking too many questions about human nature, purpose, and what makes people become who they are. An avid reader, a lover of stories, and an advocate for helping people pursue lives of meaning and purpose, he brings a voice shaped by faith, service, and thousands of conversations with people at every stage of life. Christopher lives with his wife of more than two decades and their three children, and believes that our stories are what shape who we are and how we live.

Kevin M. Linzey is a retired Army finance officer who now serves as the Finance Director for a non-profit organization in Colorado. A lover of the great outdoors, he and his family love hiking and anything on the water. Combined with his love of travel, he plans to complete the Great Loop within the next 5 years. Kevin loves reading and watching movies, and is already planning a series of stories set in a small Texas town where people are experiencing bizarre, mystical things.

Paul E. Linzey writes both fiction and nonfiction. His works can be seen on his website, www.paullinzey.com. Personal interests include music, travel, theater, digital photography, and meeting people. A former pastor, military chaplain, and university professor, he is the president of a local writers group, teaches once in a while at the church he and his wife attend, plus voluntarily leads a creative writing class at a local seniors center.

And just in case you're wondering, my co-writers listed above are my sons. I love them and am quite proud of each of them. They are so much fun to hang out with, talk with, and write with.

www.ingramcontent.com/pod-product-compliance
Lightning Source LLC
LaVergne TN
LVHW100521110826

845146LV00002B/732

* 9 7 9 8 9 9 8 5 0 6 0 9 3 *